Daring to Speak
Love's Name

Statements in support of publication:

'This book should definitely be published. It deals with so many issues that people are frightened of, and brings them into the open. Nothing but good can come from discussing the world as it really is and then trying to see what under God we can do about it'

— Reverend Malcolm Johnson,
Rector of St Botolph's Church, London,
and member of the General Synod

'I think the book is a genuinely useful piece of work and will be a good resource book for clergy who are brave enough to make use of it. Without setting out to, it serves to show people how spirituality and sexuality, honestly addressed, can travel together rather than pull apart'

— Right Reverend Richard Holloway,
Bishop of Edinburgh

'Daring to Speak Love's Name is a skilled and sensitive book which meets a pastoral need. To stop publication after its recommendation by publishers' readers of such quality inevitably raises the question of censorship, prejudice, and indeed the independence of scholarship'

— Canon Eric James,
Honorary Director of Christian Action,
and Preacher to Gray's Inn

'This book affirms that Christian, lesbian and gay people are saying to the rest of the Church, "We are here to stay. We have been given gifts. We are beginning to know how to celebrate those gifts. We intend to keep on doing so. We would like to share them with people who are not lesbian and gay and we grieve when they are refused."'

— Reverend Jim Cotter,
author and liturgist

Daring to Speak Love's Name

A GAY AND LESBIAN PRAYER BOOK

Edited by Elizabeth Stuart

HAMISH HAMILTON · LONDON

HAMISH HAMILTON

Published by the Penguin Group
Penguin Books Ltd, 27 Wrights Lane, London W8 5TZ, England
Penguin Books USA Inc., 375 Hudson Street, New York, New York 10014, USA
Penguin Books Australia Ltd, Ringwood, Victoria, Australia
Penguin Books Canada Ltd, 10 Alcorn Avenue, Toronto, Ontario, Canada M4V 3B2
Penguin Books (NZ) Ltd, 182–190 Wairau Road, Auckland 10, New Zealand

Penguin Books Ltd, Registered Offices: Harmondsworth, Middlesex, England

First published 1992
1 3 5 7 9 10 8 6 4 2

The Acknowledgements included in pp. 146–58 constitute
an extension of this copyright page

Filmset in Palatino 11/13½pt by DatIX International, Bungay, Suffolk
Printed in England by Clays Ltd, St Ives plc

A CIP catalogue record for this book is available from the British Library

ISBN 0-241-13335-1

Dedicated to
Paul Grosch, Jim Little, Anne Littlejohn,
Francesca Murphy, Gaynor Pollard, Adrian Thatcher,
Dilys Wadman
and
Judith Longman

Contents

'. . . I am true Love, I fill
The hearts of boy and girl with mutual flame.'
Then sighing said the other, 'Have thy will,
I am the Love that dare not speak its name.'

From 'Two Loves' by Lord Alfred Douglas

Preface

Liturgy is dangerous. This is what I have learnt during the last few months as I have fought to get this book published. It is an extraordinary story and one which all who read and use this book should be aware of.

This book of prayers, blessings and liturgies for lesbian and gay Christians was initially commissioned by the Society for Promoting Christian Knowledge (SPCK), a publisher of religious, theological and liturgical works highly respected in academic and ecclesiastical circles. I was delighted to be asked to compile this book as I knew that it was a much-needed resource and also because I felt it was a sign of life within the Church as a whole, a sign that the pastoral needs of lesbian and gay people were beginning to be taken seriously.

By the time the book was completed, members of the publications committee of SPCK were expressing reservations at the idea of the book. In response to this the editorial director agreed to send it to an unusually large number of distinguished readers – half of whom were chosen by the committee. Their unanimous recommendation that the book be published was clearly not what the committee wanted to hear and so they arranged for the typescript to be sent to SPCK's president, the Archbishop of Canterbury. I believe that this unprecedented involvement of Dr Carey in the publishing policy of SPCK put him in an impossible position. If he had shown indifference or admiration for the book

and the outside world had come to hear of this, he would have
been seen as giving it his approval. It would then have risked
being seen as an official publication of the Church of England –
something never intended by myself or the wide range of
contributors to the book. Dr Carey wrote to express his disapproval, particularly of the inclusion of prayers for people
affected with HIV/AIDS alongside material celebrating and affirming lesbian and gay relationships, on the pretext that it might
'foster the myth that HIV and AIDS are confined to the homosexual community'. He also threatened to resign from his presid-
ency of SPCK if he continued to be unhappy with its editorial
policy.

Unsurprisingly, the publications committee took the hint and
voted to abandon the book. A public outcry followed, with
protests by a wide range of people, including professors of
theology, bishops, authors and readers of SPCK books. Three
weeks later the negative decision was confirmed by the full
governing body of SPCK.

Why did these governors (very few of whom hold any
ecclesiastical position) feel they had the right to stop the publication of prayers for lesbian and gay people, a disparate and largely
invisible constituency, very poorly served by mainstream denominations? Lesbian and gay relationships and lives are not mirrored
in standard liturgical language or imagery in the UK – even the
need for liturgical language that does not exclude women is an
argument that has not yet permeated most congregations – and I
hoped that the book would help them to articulate their experience in worship and prayer together. I thought the book would
also be of use to clergy and Christian communities seeking to
reach out to and welcome lesbian and gay people and that
heterosexual people, particularly all those living in relationships
other than marriage, would be able to identify with some of the
feelings and hopes expressed in the book. The book was not a

manifesto for lesbian and gay rights, nor an attempt to pre-empt the long and painful debate on the subject of homosexuality that still lies ahead of all the Christian denominations in Britain. It was simply the articulation of lesbian and gay experience in prayer and liturgical rites.

It is well known that the English have difficulty in discussing matters of sex and sexuality. Traditionally, the stress has been on not offending people by talking in public about what one does in private. This attitude has meant that the silence about the reality of homosexuality has been particularly hard to break and for that reason all the more crippling for people having difficulty coming to terms with their orientation. As a result of the AIDS crisis, there has been some movement in the churches in Britain over the last decade towards taking seriously the realities of the lives of lesbians and gay men. Most good has been done by individuals and small groups of clergy or congregations becoming aware of particular needs and responding to them.

Even in the Roman Catholic Church in England and Wales the silence greeting the infamous 1986 letter from Cardinal Ratzinger, which forbade bishops and clergy to teach that the homosexual condition in itself was not sinful and ordered them to withdraw all support for self-affirming lesbian and gay Catholic groups, could be interpreted as dismay rather than approval of it. Confrontation with Rome is carefully avoided and gay Catholics are supported in private. The problem with this approach, of course, is that the public assumption that there is no place for 'practising homosexuals' within the Church goes unchallenged, which is no comfort to those alienated by the Roman position who are trying to cope with the homophobia of secular society and who assume the Church has nothing to offer.

Committees in the Methodist and United Reformed Churches have in recent years produced documents calling for gay and lesbian people to be welcomed, but these have not yet been unanimously accepted by those denominations. The Church of England in its General Synod has gone in for more confrontational debate, with calls for the recognition of the value of homosexual relationships being balanced by witch-hunts of gay clergy — encouraged by the inability of members of Synod to find a formula that could be approved of by all the opposing parties. The secular tabloid press has an insatiable appetite for the topic of homosexuality and the Church (particularly 'gay vicar' scandals), and this media interest seems to colour the positions struck in Synod. Yet, in December of last year, the House of Bishops of the General Synod issued a statement, *Issues in Human Sexuality*, which called upon congregations to find ways of welcoming lesbian and gay people into the Church and listening to their experience. This heart-warming call was tempered by the insistence that gay and lesbian relationships, whilst capable of being a blessing to those involved and those around, are inferior to marriage and by the call for lesbian and gay clergy to remain celibate. I should imagine that it will be a shock to many international readers to learn that the churches in Britain are only just beginning to acknowledge that lesbian and gay people exist. Whereas a number of Christian denominations in the United States have set up programmes to enable lesbian and gay people to have a voice in the Church and engage in dialogue with their fellow Christians, British churches are only now at the stage of considering whether lesbian and gay people should be listened to.

Nor should it be forgotten that the Church of England is the established Church and as such is looked to by the government to give moral leadership to the nation. This burden of expectation upon the Church and its leaders tends to dampen the spirit of adventure and advancement in Church circles.

Again and again the opponents of this book argued that their objections to its publication lay in the fact that it was a book of liturgies. Why do some of those who hold powerful positions in the Church find the very idea of such a book deeply threatening? For all Christians, liturgy — the public, communal and ordered gatherings of believers for the purpose of worship — is extremely important. It is the time when, through words and symbols, we celebrate and experience God's loving and transforming presence in the midst of our lives as individuals and as community and we connect our lives with those who have gone before us. For liturgy to be effective it needs to articulate and speak to the experience of those who participate in it. The unfortunate fact is that for most of its history the Church's liturgies have been written by white, middle-class men and have reflected their experience and values. Lesbian, gay and bisexual people, along with people from different races, children and many more have been deprived of a liturgical language to make sense of their experience. Linguistic deprivation is a particularly effective way of keeping people silent and disempowered.

But now we are doing it for ourselves. We have begun to articulate our spirituality, our understanding of reality in terms of our relationships and faith, in liturgical form. And it is threatening to those with power in the churches because it is an acknowledge-ment that we do not need them to help us make sense of our lives. It is also threatening because it cannot be argued with. One can enter into a debate over an academic thesis, but one cannot argue with a person's articulation of their experience. It is the expression of the heart rather than the head, and therefore it is not controllable. And it is threatening because many aspects of gay, lesbian and bisexual experience are not unique but shared by thousands of heterosexual Christians. By daring to speak love's name we expose the extent to which Church teaching and liturgy can have very little grounding in reality and become irrelevant. That is why to many who hold power and status in the Church this book is dangerous.

They cannot be allowed to win because they do not own the Church. The Church as the people of God is larger than buildings, larger than institutions, larger than hierarchies and denominations, larger than any religion. Where two or three are gathered together in God's name there is the Church. Most of the Church exists outside the structured institutions, and rightly so, for Christ came and worked in the world – not in temples or ivory towers. He taught people to find God in the daily round of their ordinary lives, in places where the religious establishment believed God to be absent. It is for this reason that I have now chosen a non-religious publisher for *Daring to Speak Love's Name*. I want it to be read and used by people who are quite rightly suspicious of the institutional churches and their attempts to manipulate and control the reality of people's lives and relationships. The editorial department at Hamish Hamilton immediately grasped the importance of this book and the need that exists for it, whilst representatives of the institutional churches within SPCK could see only the threat the book posed to them and their power and status. By being so clearly and publicly rejected by the self-appointed guardians of the established Church, the book has been freed to speak to a wider audience. There is now no danger of this book being mistaken for an official publication of any Christian denomination, but it is by and for the Church. Christian leaders, no matter what their tradition, will be unable to ignore it.

And yet, despite all this, and the negative decision made by SPCK's governors, what I have been left with is an overwhelming sense that the tide has turned. The opposition to the book, within the churches and within society as a whole, was so limited and uninformed, their arguments so weak, and the support for the publication of the book was so widespread. The Holy Spirit is winging its way through prejudice, fear, indifference and the awful spectre of fundamentalism to lead God's people forward towards the day when lesbian and gay people are welcomed into all Christian communities and celebrated for who they are.

This book is the first of its kind to be published in Britain. There have been a number of similar works published in the United States, where groups of marginalized Christians have been writing their own liturgy for some time. They have been quicker to recognize that they too are the Church and that God's spirit lives and moves among them, helping them to articulate their experience in words and ritual. And Church leaders have been forced to pay attention to that experience at least. Because experiential liturgy is still in its infancy among the lesbian and gay Christian community in Britain, I have had to draw a lot of material from American sources. As far as I am aware, however, there is nothing quite like this book available yet even in the USA. Lesbian and gay Christians are, I believe, naturally ecumenical. We still have too few friends to be able to afford to reject people on doctrinal grounds. We know we need each other and we naturally learn from one another. I hope this book will help to sustain and develop the grass-roots ecumenical process going on among the lesbian and gay Christian community, a process which in its sincerity and success puts the 'official' process to shame.

This book is a celebration of friendship and the product of friendship. Sally Abbey, Fiona McMorrough and the staff of Hamish Hamilton stepped in to rescue the book after SPCK abandoned it. I have been deeply moved by their understanding of its importance and commitment to it. No religious publisher could have produced it better or dared to own it with as much pride.

Dr Elizabeth Stuart, 1992

Foreword

Giving the title *Daring to Speak Love's Name* to this gay and lesbian prayer book seems designed to set my heterosexual, patriarchal and normatively normal teeth on edge. For the sensitive, passionate and provocative commentary of Elizabeth Stuart and the documents which she has collected together are not about 'love' in general but about specifically homosexual love. Is this not another example of the imperialism of the lesbians and gay men who 'do protest too much'? Having laid claim to a lively and lovely adjective like 'gay', they seem now to be making some dominant claim for the idea of 'love' and certainly for the concept of 'friendship'. Love, friendship and gaiety are, surely, universally human traits, activities, possibilities.

However, it is precisely these issues that this book is about. Yes – love, friendship and gaiety are universally human possibilities and promises. Why are the attitudes, moral rules and supportive structures reinforcing and promoting them not easily and equally available to all – heterosexuals and homosexuals? The Christian churches bless marriage. Why do they seem, too often, to curse homosexual friendships and commitments which strive to be one to one, permanent, responsible and desirous of recognition and support? (See, for example, the poignantly revealing phrases on page 22 about 'able to bless those whom others refuse to recognize as blessed and may even perceive to be cursed'.)

One of the reasons which was given for the SPCK (as at least a quasi-official institution of the Church of England) not publishing this book was that some of the liturgies and prayers offered in it seem to claim the same status for homosexual commitments and covenants as for marriage. This is specifically denied in the book. What these liturgies reflect is a wistful longing for some sort of acceptance and public recognition, including the blessing of the Church, which promotes the possibilities of stability, responsibility and permanance which marriage enjoys — or should enjoy. It seems to me that there is much in this book which could help all of us who are concerned to reassert the values of responsibility, long-term commitment and mutual friendship, with respect to all serious interpersonal relationships, whether in marriage or society at large. Indeed, I find it ironic, moving and challenging that the documents in this book should reflect a longing for liturgical, corporate and prayerful response to so many aspects of human living together. I judge the book to be quite correct in reminding, for example, us who are pastors and priests that the pastoral and liturgical ministry of the Church is too much confined to 'hatching, matching and despatching' and does not mesh with many of life's significant joyful and challenging occasions. We tend to fail in ministering to those who, for one reason or another, are not caught up in married and family life.

It seems to me, therefore, that this book gives those of us outside the lesbian and gay communities a moving insight into what life is like for them. It presents us with a series of challenges which could foster a more open and sensitive approach to such matters as the responsible disciplining of sexuality and the importance of long-term supportive relationships. It is also, and in its own intentions primarily, an offer of encouragement and support to hopeful and enjoyable life together for homophiles in what is still a very cold climate.

This book sets out its agenda only at its very beginning and raises many issues which call for further discussion. What, for example, are the implications and long-term status of the remark on page 8: 'Our sexuality is the seat of our relationality'? Is this so? Or does this view reflect an over-obsessive concern with sexuality in its narrow, genital sense? Such questions can be properly answered only once we have faced up to, and found our way through, the oppressive domination of current social mores about heterosexuality and patriarchal families to which this book draws attention. Then there is the remark on page 82 about 'coming into the lesbian and gay community which is their community'. Surely the human community, the local community, the neighbourly community, is the community of all of us. But, once again, this book gives evidence to the contrary and challenges us to find ways of overcoming the present necessary defensiveness of very particularly defined communities so that our differences may be no longer defensively asserted but recognized and shared in coordinated and creative ways.

So this book has much to offer us all as we seek within the Church, and for society at large, to reassert and renew our understanding of the central importance of human relationships that, with joy and hope, take seriously the possibilities of long-term and responsible friendship. It challenges us to work out afresh the proper place of sexuality *within* those relationships and friendships. It also reminds us that these relationships include not only the friendship and mutuality within marriage and the family, but also a variety of other mutually respected and accepted ways of covenanting and bonding between particular persons for the sustenance, promotion and sharing of gaiety, friendship and love.

Rt Revd Dr David Jenkins
3 June 1992

Acknowledgements

John Breslin, Dudley Cave, Malcolm Johnson, Ann Peart and Neil Thomas generously agreed to share their considerable experience of ministering to those marginalized on the grounds of their sexuality and relationships. My partner, Jane Robson, cast her critical eye over the manuscript at every stage of its development. It is a great joy to me that this book should appear in the same year that we celebrate ten years together.

Juliet Doswell undertook the laborious and thankless task of checking references and extracts. Richard Kirker of the Lesbian and Gay Christian Movement was responsible for the idea of this book and for suggesting that I should write it. He encouraged and nagged me at every stage in its development. Richard provided invaluable help and advice when it became clear that SPCK was going to drop the book. I could not have had better support.

There are many others who must be thanked for publicly and privately supporting the book when attempts were being made to suppress it. I cannot mention them all, but would like particularly to acknowledge the support of the following: the Bishops of Durham, Edinburgh, Crediton, St Andrews, Monmouth; Professors Peter Selby, Chris Rowland, Morna Hooker, Leslie Houlden; Canon Eric James; the Revds Dr Anthony Phillips, Jim Cotter, Trevor Beeson, Michael Peet, Tony Crowe, David Randall, Peter O'Driscoll, Robert Evans, Dr Jeffrey John, John Peirce, Martin

Kelly, Bruce Kinsey, Dr David Stacey, Bernard Lynch, Andrew Deuchar, Keith Trivasse and Roz Hunt; Margaret Orr Deas, Janet Morley, Monica Furlong, Ruth McCurry, Sara Maitland, Catherine Treasure, Alison Webster, Elaine Willis, Elizabeth Templeton, Eva Heymann, Martin Pendergast, Sebastian Sandys, Dr Stephen Barton, Austin Allen, Guy Denman, Penny Cassell, Jo Watson, Helen Harman, Matthew Sexton, Julie Taylor, Alistair Marshall, Catherine South, Patrick Gilbert; the hundreds of people who wrote to me and to SPCK expressing support for the book; my students who kept me going when I was ready to give up the fight; and my family who do not like what I do but love me anyway. Any merits this book has are due to this 'coalition of justice-seeking friends' (to use Mary Hunt's phrase) and to them I offer my deepest thanks.

This book is firstly dedicated to my colleagues in the Theology and Philosophy subject group at the College of St Mark and St John. Over the past five years Adrian Thatcher, Paul Grosch, Gaynor Pollard, Jim Little, Anne Littlejohn, Francesca Murphy and Dilys Wadman have inspired, encouraged and supported me. They have created a safe space for me to dare to speak love's name. Their friendship sustains me from day to day.

Secondly this book is dedicated to Judith Longman, who originally asked me to write it and offered constant encouragement, advice and constructive criticism. She has been a good friend to me and to the book and I hope that she now feels that her long and hard fight to have this book published was not in vain.

Introduction

> Whoever abides in friendship abides in God, and God in them
> ... God is friendship.

So wrote Aelred, the twelfth-century Abbot of Rievaulx, in his work *De Spirituali Amicitia* ('On Spiritual Friendship').[1] His work, written as a contribution to the medieval discussion on the nature of friendship, stands out as the fullest, most original volume on the subject. The Christian tradition had long idealized 'Platonic friendship', a purely spiritual, as opposed to physical, relationship, but Aelred saw such dualistic distinctions between the flesh and the spirit as false. He broke a monastic taboo by allowing his monks to develop 'particular friendships' and, within the bounds of celibacy, he encouraged the physical expression of affection. Aelred believed that true friendship, whether expressed in an overtly sexual manner or not, was the relationship that taught us most about God's love for us. It is the relationship in which we experience the continuity between God and ourselves most directly, for 'God is friendship'.

Aelred's most important contribution to the theology of friendship was his steadfast refusal to condemn its physical, even sexual, expression. He discouraged sexual relations among his monks, whether homosexual or heterosexual, simply because they had taken a vow to abstain from such behaviour, but he acknowledged that great joy could be experienced in a sexual relationship which could enrich the friendship and teach the lovers something deeper about God's love for them. I think that *Daring to Speak Love's Name* is a book that Aelred would have approved of, for it is a celebration of loving friendship and it is grounded in a theology of friendship.

The Theology of Friendship

What is friendship? It is a relationship entered into *freely* by two or more people. It is a relationship based upon the recognition of a *fundamental equality* between the participants. It is a relationship based upon *love and acceptance* of the participants as they are. Friendship is *empowering, affirming* and *challenging* for those involved. Friendship can *cut across social barriers*. Friendships are therefore *inclusive* rather then exclusive relationships. Friendship is *political* when it motivates people to come together to change structures and situations which damage and diminish their friends.

'God is friendship,' wrote Aelred. This is expressed most clearly in the Christian doctrine of the Trinity. God though one, is a relationship of three persons, a relationship based upon equality, mutuality and interdependence, as well as a celebration and affirmation of diversity. In *De Trinitate* St Augustine examined the definition of the Trinity as lover, the beloved and the love. The Trinity is a creative, sustaining and saving relationship that reaches out beyond itself. It is a relationship that includes and celebrates embodiment. The whole of creation is made to exist in friendship. Species are interdependent but once human beings reject friendship and respect for creation, and allow dominance, exploitation and selfish misuse, the whole system breaks down.

Our planet is dying because we ceased to be her friend and became her enemy. Species are being wiped out because we see them not as friends but as objects for human use. When friendship dies, part of each friend begins to die.

According to the oldest creation account (Genesis 2.18), God creates humankind for friendship: 'It is not good that the man should be alone; I will make him a helper as his partner'. (Being a 'helper' did not imply subordination – God is often referred to as humanity's helper.) Sin corrupts that relationship into enmity and unequal power relations between the sexes (Genesis 3.15). In the later creation story humankind is created in God's own image and that means it is created to be in relation, in right relation with itself, God and the rest of the planet, a relationship of friendship (Genesis 1.27). That friendship includes awe and respect for God and each other. In neither of these accounts of creation are sexuality or sexual intercourse associated with sin or corruption. It is assumed that the friendship between men and women may include sexual relations. Passion and sexual love are not necessarily antithetical to friendship. Of course, as the oldest creation account acknowledges, we are all prone to sin. It is easy for passion to become corrupted by self-centredness, and for jealousy and possessiveness to distort the underlying friendship. But when these emotions are overcome passionate friendship between human beings is a reflection of the passionate friendship of God for humanity.

The prophet Hosea saw that God's love for humanity was a passionate love which desired right relation with a ferocity and intensity that could only be compared with a lover's. Isaiah knew that God would not 'divorce' his people (50.1). And, like a lover's, God's passion is embodied; right relation must be expressed in concrete, physical ways, in working for justice and peace. It is never a purely spiritual phenomenon. Humanity is created to be in relationship with God. This is a relationship based not upon domination, control or fear but upon mutual respect, concern, love, justice, forgiveness and interdependence. Humanity needs God in order to be truly human and God has chosen to entrust the world to humanity. Sin, the failure to exist in right relation, disturbs and damages the friendship between humans and also the friendship between God and humanity, but God forgives and starts again and encourages us to do the same.

Christians believe that in the person of Jesus of Nazareth the image of God shines out with a force and clarity unparalleled in the history of humanity, so that we can say: 'In him was God' or, 'He was God made flesh'. It comes as no surprise, then, to learn that his life, his teaching and his death were rooted in friendship. Jesus appears to announce the imminent arrival of God's reign on earth. It is a reign that will be characterized by right relations between human beings – there will be no rich, powerful dominant class on whom the rest are dependent for survival, all will be equal because all will acknowledge their absolute dependence upon God and each other. This is the theme behind the Sermon on the Mount (Matthew 5–7), the Magnificat (Luke 1.47–55) and the words of Isaiah that, according to Luke, Jesus reads at the beginning of his ministry. '. . . he has anointed me to bring good news to the poor. He has sent me to proclaim release to the captives and recovery of sight to the blind, to let the oppressed go free, to proclaim the year of the Lord's favour' (Luke 4.18–19).

Jesus therefore had to convince the rich and powerful to let go of false idols. He also had to convince the powerless, the non-persons, the poor, the women, the children, the 'sinners', the 'unclean', the sick, that God was their friend and on their side. To make God's friendship real to them he became one of them, he lived among them, ate with them (a most important sign of intimate friendship), touched them, healed them, forgave them and defended them. He treated them as persons made in the image of God. It was amongst these people that the reign of

God began because they acknowledged their need for friendship and their dependence upon God and each other. They had nothing to lose. The powerful had everything to lose: their security, comfort, status, good name, influence. Jesus asked them to become as children, as nobodies. A few realized that God's society founded upon friendship would be worth it, most did not. Some were so threatened by the whole idea that they wanted Jesus dead.

We may not know much for certain about the historical Jesus but we do know that he had friends. These friendships were based upon mutual acceptance and love, and they cut across religious and social divisions. The friendships were empowering, creative and healing. They were also challenging, and sometimes confrontational, and had significance beyond themselves because they formed the nucleus of the coming reign of God. Jesus dies because of his friendships, because they rocked and undermined the political and religious systems of the day. Power is usually gained and sustained by dividing people against each other, creating castes and subcastes, clean and unclean, men and women, righteous and sinners and so on. Friendship undermines all that. It acknowledges no barriers and locates the dignity of each person in their being, not in their status, in *who* they are, not *what* they are. Jesus dies for his friends and for God's friendship with humanity. It is a passionate act. It seems that power has defeated friendship, but God vindicates Jesus and raises him to new life. His Spirit continues to bind together in right relation unlikely friends. And the powerful still find it threatening.

Very quickly in its history the Church tended to adopt a dualistic attitude to matter and spirit, to natural (the earthy and physical: bad) and supernatural (the unworldly and spiritual: good). The natural (naturally sinful and dangerous) had to be subdued and tamed. Our bodies were regarded as dirty and repulsive to God, and sexual union was solely for the purposes of procreation within the bounds of marriage. Women continued to be associated with the earthly and sexual, with unruly 'nature', and therefore had to be controlled, dominated and contained. The predominant understanding of God became first the absolute, unknowable being and then tyrant ruler or fearful judge, friend of the powerful, who had placed each person within a carefully ordered and divided society. Once Church and State had formed alliances, to question the way society was run or the rightness of the relationships fostered was to question God. First celibacy and then, after the Reformation, marriage became the ideal Christian way; neither was based upon a theology of friendship.

Two groups of people have recently sought to revive the concept of friendship as the fundamental and ideal relationship between God and humanity, among human persons, and between human beings and the rest of creation. This is not to say that they are the first to develop a theology of friendship, or that friendships are only possible within these two groups. But the emphasis they put upon equality and mutuality as the foundations upon which all relationships should be built stands in contrast to the dominant tradition in Christianity, which has defined relationships in hierarchical terms.

The first group is the Christian feminists. The feminist movement has exposed the way in which patriarchal structures in society and the Church actually conspire to inhibit women from forming true friendships.[2] Women have internalized myths such as the one upon which patriarchy is built, that women need to love and serve men in order to be complete, whole, fulfilled human beings. This has led to competitive relationships with other women in the desperate scramble to get and keep a man. But there have always been women who have managed to form true friendships in spite of these structures and it was out of this experience of the sustaining, transforming, liberating and creative dimensions of women's friendship that the feminist movement was born. Women experienced what it meant to be saved – to be born again as a person of dignity and worth, with the power, working alongside others, to change things. Christian feminists were able to peel away centuries of patriarchal interpretation of the Hebrew Scriptures and the New Testament to find a God of friendship who calls all creation into friendship. They found a forgotten and hidden history of women within the Church which disproved the assertion that women had 'always' been regarded and treated in a certain way, as part of its unchallengeable and unchangeable Christian tradition. Just as Jesus challenged the people of his day to learn new ways of relating to one another, so feminists challenge men and women to surrender the long-held structures, thought processes, theology and philosophy of patriarchy to become friends with each other and with the rest of creation. We have a choice: cling on to power and the defence of power and destroy each other and the world, or become friends and start building God's world.

The second group responsible for the reviving of the theology of friendship consists of gay men and lesbian women. They too have been silenced and made invisible by patriarchy for they challenge its foundations. In a society and Church where marriage and 'the family' are still idealized and promoted as the 'norm', gay men and lesbian women have been marginalized, demonized, feared and persecuted. They too have often internalized the fear and hatred of their kind.

St Aelred was a man with strong homosexual inclinations. He seems to have had sexual relations with men before he became a monk and later fell in love with two of his fellow monks.[3] He was lucky to live in a time when Church and State were demonstrating relative tolerance for homosexual relationships. These periods of toleration are now forgotten and denied by Church authorities, who often use 'unerring' tradition as a means of dismissing gay and lesbian requests to have their stories and experiences listened to. Aelred does not seem to have questioned the validity, goodness and blessedness of his relationships. He discovered and developed his theology of friendship through them. This is remarkable when one considers the knowledge about human sexuality in general and homosexuality in particular that is now available to us, but which Aelred was ignorant of: the discovery that some people are naturally oriented emotionally and sexually towards members of their own sex; the recognition by many, though not all, psychologists and psychiatrists that homosexuality is not a disease or disorder (a recognition that has led the World Health Organization and the associations of British and American psychiatrists to remove homosexuality from the list of mental disorders); and the probability that most of us are neither exclusively gay/lesbian nor exclusively, heterosexual but contain within us a spectrum of sexuality, parts of which can dominate at different parts of our lives.[4] Aelred seems to have realized that our sexuality is the seat of our relationality, the part of ourselves which enables us to relate to the rest of the world. It determines how we relate to God, friends, lovers, art, animals, nature and so on. Therefore, to declare someone's sexuality to be disordered is to declare all their relationships disordered. It is to say that he or she does not bear the image of God and to condemn them to loneliness, isolation and despair, to deprive them of life. Aelred believed that his sexuality had led him to God — it was not disordered. A disordered sexuality is one that manifests itself in the exploitation and abuse of others and heterosexual people are equally likely to manifest such disordered behaviour as gay or lesbian people.

Just as there have always been women who have enjoyed and celebrated their womanhood as coming from and leading to God, so there have always been lesbians and gay men who have trusted their feelings enough to reject the overpowering condemnation by society and Church in order to discover the presence of God in their friendships. Although some gay and lesbian lovers have internalized the idealization of marriage to such a degree that they have felt the need to model their own relationships on it, with rigid division of roles, many gay and lesbian people, highly suspicious of marriage, prefer to understand and work out their relationships in terms of friendship. Lesbian and gay theologians have gone back to the Bible and found that passages used to condemn their love are based upon the belief that people committing homosexual acts are always acting against nature, a belief not supported by modern science. They have discovered the celebration in highly erotic terms of the same-sex love between David and Jonathan. They have noted the concern that Jesus manifested to those who were considered to have fallen short of a sexual ideal, to be habitual sexual sinners, dangerous to be around, and undeserving of full civil rights (all of which applied to women in Jesus' day) and they claim the same love and affirmation that Jesus gave to the outcasts of his day. With these 'little ones' of Jesus' time they affirm their dignity and worth as people created in the image of God and the manifestation of that image in their deepest relationships.[5]

The experience of gay men and lesbians can teach the rest of humanity that friendship can be expressed and nourished sexually. Those engaged in sexual relations, whether heterosexual or homosexual, do not need to sacrifice equality and mutuality. Of course, many heterosexual couples have come to realize that the secret of a happy marriage or relationship is friendship between the partners but the fact is that, historically, marriage has been used as a means of dominating women and that in a patriarchal society laws, customs, religion and culture all tend to conspire to prevent true friendship between men and women blossoming. Whilst it is important to avoid idealizing them, women's friendships, same-sex sexual relationships and non-sexual friendships do challenge this system and offer other models of relating for which the world should be grateful.

Friendship and Liturgy

Describing her experience of a lesbian relationship the poet Adrienne Rich writes:

> we're out in a country that has no language
> no laws, we're chasing the raven and the wren
> through gorges unexplored since dawn
> whatever we do together is pure invention
> the maps they gave us were out of date
> by years . . .[6]

Depriving people of language with which to make sense of their experience is a particularly effective way of keeping them silent and disempowered. For centuries the dominant language expressed the experiences of women and of gay and lesbian people in terms of sin, perversion, temptation and guilt. We are only just beginning to find our own voices and language to articulate the language of friendship. Of course the Christian liturgy has reflected the dominant values of the institutional church and society. 'Liturgy', literally the 'people's work', is used to describe the public, communal and ordered gatherings of Christians for the purpose of worship. In coming together Christians remind themselves and others that we are part of a community, that salvation is not an individual matter but a community experience. We are reminded of how we belong to one another and repent of our failure to live this out in practice. We are comforted, inspired and challenged by being reminded, through the reading of the Scriptures, that we stand in continuity with a historical community which experienced healing and liberation through the God who now travels with us and has promised (in the words of Julian of Norwich) that 'all shall be well and all shall be well, and all manner of thing shall be well'. Through the use of words and, more importantly, symbols, which manage to express realities which words cannot articulate, as individuals and community we experience God's grace — the healing, transforming, liberating, unconditional love that so many encountered in the person of Jesus of Nazareth. Liturgy offers us the time and space and inspiration to connect our lives and history with that of other lives and God's life. For the liturgy to be effective it needs to articulate and speak to the experience of those who take part in it, in word and symbol. The fact is that for lesbian and gay people, many women, and all those many people living in relationships other than happy marriages, the Church's liturgy, certainly within all the major Christian denominations, often fails to articulate or even take account of their experience. And while Church authorities continue to condemn homosexual relationships, or see them as inferior and hold up marriage as the ideal, there is little hope that the central liturgies will be altered. This deprivation does not only affect those marginalized; the whole body of Christ is impoverished and rendered less effective when parts of it are frozen out, ignored, denied. And many clergy who want to minister effectively also feel the pain of liturgical deprivation.

In the account of Jesus' resurrection in John's Gospel, Mary Magdalene finding the tomb empty runs to tell Jesus' disciples. Peter and the mysterious 'other' or 'beloved' disciple run together to the tomb. The other disciple reaches the tomb first but waits for Peter to go in before him. Peter goes in, looks at the folded cloth, but does not seem to realize what has happened; the other disciple then goes in, 'and he saw and believed' (20.8). This continues a theme that runs throughout the gospel: Peter gets most things wrong, the beloved disciple gets everything right. He has to show Peter and the rest of the disciples what Jesus and his ministry is all about. Peter, of course, came to be regarded as the leader of the Church and I think that this passage teaches us a valuable lesson, namely that the Church authorities come to understand the truth only because others have understood before them and passed the understanding on. Peter frequently misunderstood; he made terrible mistakes which hurt Jesus deeply. He even collaborated in his saviour's destruction by denying him. So we should not be surprised that the Church makes mistakes, some of which cause immense suffering. The Church, like Peter, needs beloved disciples to save it from denying and betraying Christ. Also significant is the fact that in all four gospels it is to women that Jesus appears first. Those marginalized by the rules of the religious establishment are the first to experience the resurrection, the first to be entrusted with the good news. Because they needed it they would believe it.

History teaches us that praxis always precedes theory. Real change, particularly in the Church, comes from the bottom up. Jesus knew this. He knew that the foundations of God's commonwealth would be built by those with no position to lose, with only friendship to offer each other. The Christian feminist movement learnt this lesson over thirty years ago and began to formulate its own language, its own liturgies, its own theology. It became 'Church' for many women. This movement has been ignored, condemned, ridiculed and dismissed by many representatives of the institutional churches, yet now some of them, like Peter before the tomb, are coming to value women's experience and the truths expressed in feminist theology.

The modern gay and lesbian liberation movement within Christianity is only just beginning to dare to speak love's name in liturgical settings, we are only just beginning to be 'Church' for each other, only just beginning to develop a theology of liberation for ourselves. This book offers the first fruits of this process. It is offered to several groups of people. First and foremost it is offered to gay and lesbian Christians to help them to speak love's name, both in the day-to-day round of their lives and at its turning points. The book is also offered to those who wish to minister effectively to lesbian and gay people and seek the words and symbols with which to do so. The wisdom of five ministers experienced in this area are offered as guidance to other ministers. The book is offered also to those many people who would not wish to define themselves as lesbian or gay but who would consider a same-sex friendship or friendships to be their primary relationship/s. I hope this book will enable these people to speak about their relationships before God. The book is also for heterosexual Christians, married or in non-married partnerships, who feel that their love or experience of love is not named in the language of Christian worship as offered by the churches. And finally, this book is offered to all Christians, that they may learn about the gay and lesbian experience of love and friendship and be enriched by it, perhaps identify with some of it, and reach out in friendship to their gay and lesbian brothers and sisters.

Whilst this book was being written, the House of Bishops of the General Synod of the Church of England published a statement, *Issues in Human Sexuality*. There appeared to be much in this report to warm the hearts of gay and lesbian Christians. The bishops apologized for the Church's prejudice, ignorance and oppression in dealing with homosexuality in the past; they steadfastly refused to label homosexuality or gay and lesbian relationships as sinful; and, whilst insisting that homosexual relations are always inferior to the ideal of heterosexual marriage and that gay and lesbian clergy must give witness to the ideal and therefore remain celibate, they counselled respect for the integrity of those lesbians and gay men, lay or ordained, who believe their sexual relationships to be right in the sight of God. Most importantly, in section 4:7, the bishops drew attention to the need for 'congregations to be places of open acceptance and friendship for homophiles as for people of every kind, both generally and in such settings as the best sort of house group'. They also called upon the Church to listen to its 'gay and lesbian brothers and sisters'. I hope this book will help to fulfil the vision of the statement.

Mary Hunt sums all this up when she argues that we need to 'sacramentalize friendship': 'To sacramentalize is to pay attention. It is what a community does when it names and claims ordinary human experiences as holy, connecting them with history and propelling them into the future.'[7]

The material in this book is offered as example and inspiration. It is offered to be adapted, rearranged, rewritten and supplemented to speak to particular situations and needs. By no means all of the material has been written by or for lesbian and gay people. Lesbian and gay people share experiences and concerns with many other groups of people. Using prayers and readings first written for other situations serves to remind gay and lesbian people of our interconnectedness with other people and our need to work with all who labour for liberation. This is how all Christians use the Bible. Written in times very different from our own and addressing situations and issues often no longer relevant, the Scriptures still have a power to move, comfort, inspire and challenge us, because there is something in our experience which allows us to relate and identify with the situation, preoccupations and concerns of the original authors. Sometimes words, symbols and actions fail to express feelings or experience, and we can only rest in silence with each other and God. Sometimes we become so busy in worship that we fail to hear the Spirit moving among us. Silence should be an important part of all Christian worship and should be incorporated into the liturgical material offered here.

This book is not intended to encourage gay men and lesbians to leave 'the Church'. Men and women, homosexual and heterosexual, belong to one another, need each other and have to learn to live and work together. But it takes strength and courage to live and work and worship with other Christians who do not seem to want you, cannot accept you, and who condemn you. That strength and courage can only come from being with those who do love you, who do affirm you, who do understand. Gay and lesbian Christians need to meet, pray with and minister to each other in order to be empowered to cope with rejection, condemnation or devaluing of their relationships elsewhere. The history of Christianity is the history of different groups of people with different traditions, beliefs and practices who form the mass that we label 'Church'. The trouble begins when one group claims exclusive right to the title and shuts out all those who will not conform to its model. In the Celtic tradition of Christianity, which long resisted the attempts to conform its teaching and practice to the Roman model, the Holy Spirit is not represented as a white dove, tame and pure, but by a wild goose. Geese are not controllable, they make a lot of noise and have a habit of biting those who try and contain them. Geese fly faster and further in a flock than on their own. They also make excellent 'guard dogs'. Gay and lesbian Christians know that God's spirit is not a tame dove but a wild goose, free of ecclesiastical attempts to control and confine it, that makes its home in the most unlikely places. The Spirit comes not in quiet conformity but demanding to be heard. And its song is not sweet to many. This Spirit drives people together, demanding that they support and travel with each other. And it often forces those on whom it rests to become noisy, passionate and courageous guardians of the gospel. I hope this book will enable gay and lesbian people to make a noise which will attract others out of their isolation into the flock. I hope that the noise grows until other Christians can no longer ignore the flapping of the wings. I hope that it will not take too long before the whole flock is daring to speak, sing and dance love's name.

1

Celebrating Lesbian
and Gay Relationships

We have blessed fields when crops were planted, houses when
newly occupied, pets in honour of Saint Francis, and even the
hounds at a Virginia fox hunt. We have blessed MX missiles
called 'Peacemakers' and warships whose sole purpose was to
kill and destroy, calling them, in at least one instance, *Corpus
Christi* – the body of Christ. Why would it occur to us to
withhold our blessing from a human relationship that produces
a more complete person in each of the partners, because of
their life together?[1]

Despite the convincing logic of Bishop Spong and other theologians, there is a tremendous resistance among our main Christian
denominations to the idea that the churches should offer gay and
lesbian people the opportunity to affirm and celebrate their
primary relationships in public, liturgical ceremonies. This resistance extends to hostility to State recognition of homosexual
partnerships such as now exists in Denmark and in parts of the
United States.

However, many gay and lesbian Christians share with their
heterosexual brothers and sisters a strong desire to give thanks
to God for their primary relationship, to ask God's blessing on
their love and life together and to seek recognition and support
for the relationship from their Christian community and wider
circle of friends. Despite the official opposition of Church hierarchies and many members of congregations to the development

of such ceremonies, an enormous amount of liturgical material for the blessing and celebrating of gay and lesbian relationships has been produced in the last thirty years – written either by clergy who have had the courage to respond to this pastoral need or by the partners themselves.

Very few lesbian and gay people would want to describe these ceremonies and the relationships they celebrate as 'marriages'. Some would want to disassociate themselves from an institution which historically has been based upon structural and legalized inequality, specific gender roles, and which seems to impose at least a degree of conformity and uniformity and unrealistic expectations on those who enter it. And, of course, as a modern institution marriage seems to be in a state of grave crisis – even though very many marriages are happy and successful. From a theological perspective as well, gay and lesbian relationships cannot be described as 'marriages'. The Church of England's *Alternative Service Book* defines marriage in the following way:

The Scriptures teach us that marriage is a gift of God in creation and a means of his grace, a holy mystery in which man and woman become one flesh. It is God's purpose that, as husband and wife give themselves to each other in love throughout their lives, they shall be united in that love as Christ is united with his Church ... It is given that they may have children and be blessed in caring for them and bringing them up in accordance with God's will, to his praise and glory.

Marriage is a relationship between a man and a woman, generative in character, which traditionally represents the relationship of Christ to the Church. Whereas it is perfectly possible for lesbian and gay relationships to fulfil the other purposes of marriage given in the *ASB* – mutual comfort, bodily union and the building up of community – they cannot fulfil all these criteria for they are not between members of opposite genders, the relationships are not generative in character and they have never been symbolic representations of Christ's relationship to his Church. None of the major Christian denominations have ever found themselves able to state that lesbian and gay relationships are marriages or are equivalent to marriage, and most lesbian and gay Christians would agree. Marriage is a social, spiritual and historical institution for heterosexual men and women only; gay and lesbian relationships are very different. Healthy and mature lesbian and gay relationships do not ape marriage. Many Christians would want to say that homosexual partnerships are inferior to the ideal of marriage – the Church of England bishops state this in their recent report. Gay and lesbian Christians may want to dispute this, on the grounds that relationships should be judged on the basis of quality of the friendship between the partners, not on conformity to traditional institutions. But bishops and gay men and lesbians agree on this very important point: lesbian and gay relationships are not marriages and their celebrations are not weddings.

In my experience, most gay and lesbian people use the language of friendship when speaking about their primary relationships. 'Friendship' suggests a relationship of equals who delight in each other's company and have concern for each other's wellbeing. 'Friendship' also conjures up images of inclusivity rather than exclusivity. Most of our important relationships can be described as 'friendships' and so our most important relationship becomes part of the network of friendship which sustains and nourishes us. The concept of friendship also admits diversity, and gay and lesbian relationships are nothing if not diverse. Free from the historical model of marriage, gay and lesbian people are able to structure their primary relationships in a way that allows those involved most opportunity to grow and develop to emotional maturity in each other's love. The liturgies celebrating gay and lesbian relationships reflect these diverse needs. Many will not feel able to make life-long commitments, others will want to;

some will not wish or be able to live together, others will regard living together as an essential part of sharing their lives. The level and detail of commitment will be unique to each relationship.

So we are not talking about celebrating gay/lesbian marriages but constructing services of affirmation and blessing, or covenants of friendship, or celebrations of love – the language is important.

In *Issues in Human Sexuality* the bishops of the Church of England were anxious to stress the similarities between homosexual and heterosexual people in their emotional experiences. Both fall in love, tend to long for close, often exclusive, relationships with another person and desire to express love and commitment by mutual physical self-giving and enjoyment. Both are capable of shallow, immature, selfish and cruel relationships but 'equally among both there are those who grow steadily in fidelity and in mutual caring, understanding and support, whose partnerships are a blessing to the world around them, and who achieve great, even heroic sacrifice and devotion'.[2]

Having come to recognize that gay and lesbian relationships can be blessed, and that mutual, creative and empowering gay and lesbian relationships need just as much support and nourishment as heterosexual relationships, the bishops might have been expected to recommend the introduction of official liturgies celebrating and affirming such committed partnerships. They do not because they fear that the institution of marriage, which they continue to regard as the Christian ideal, would be undermined by such official ecclesiastical support for lesbian and gay relationships. But it would now be hard for the bishops to object to gay and lesbian people celebrating their own relationships and creating their own liturgies for that purpose.

Covenants

For anyone rooted in the Judaeo-Christian tradition, the term 'covenant' will be a familiar one. A covenant is a bond, entered into voluntarily, by which the parties make certain pledges to each other. In the ancient world it was usual for covenants to be ritually sealed and a lasting memorial to the covenant set up. Covenants tended to be made between people of unequal status, such as a vassal and his lord, but the Hebrew Scriptures refer to those with whom God makes covenants as God's friends (Exodus 33.11, Isaiah 41.8). Friendship, not a relationship of dominance and dependence, is the fundamental relationship in God's order. This is confirmed by the words of Jesus to his disciples shortly before his death: 'You are my friends if you do what I command you. I do not call you servants any longer, because the servant does not know what the master is doing; but I have called you friends, because I have made known to you everything that I have heard from my Father' (John 15.14–15). For a Christian the primordial covenant is that made between God and the people of Israel, brought to fulfilment in the person of Jesus Christ. All other covenants made in the name of God must endeavour to reflect something of the commitment that God makes to us: 'a God merciful and gracious, slow to anger, and abounding in steadfast love and faithfulness, keeping steadfast love for the thousandth generation, forgiving iniquity and transgression and sin' (Exodus 34.6–7). So friends making a covenant together will be making a serious, long-term commitment to each other and the promises they make will reflect that level of commitment. The Hebrew scriptures furnish us with two models of same-sex friendships which are solemnized with covenant pledges – David and Jonathan (1 and 2 Samuel) and Ruth and Naomi in the Book of Ruth.

Such covenants do not, of course, have to involve sexual relations and they can be made between more than two people. Because of the level of commitment involved, covenants of friendship will usually be made by people very sure of their relationship and their commitment to it.

Blessings

When a man and woman get married in a church, the priest or minister does not marry them: they marry each other – the Church simply blesses the marriage. That is to say that, through its official representative, the Church affirms that it recognizes the presence of God's grace in the relationship and pledges its support. Even though there may be reluctance to confer official blessing upon gay and lesbian relationships until the mind of the whole Church is made up on the issue, some of the basic communities of people within it may feel willing and able to bless those whom others refuse to recognize as blessed and may even perceive to be cursed.

In the Hebrew tradition all creation is the expression of the extravagant, unconditional, gracious, loving nature of the creator. When human beings co-operate with God in the continuing act of creation by treating each other with the respect and love due to beings created in the image of a loving, just God, then we say their relationships and actions are blessed. When we recognize a relationship as blessed, we are affirming that we recognize the presence of God in that relationship, bringing order out of chaos, life out of death, wholeness out of brokenness. We recognize the mysterious power of divine love operating between the people involved and flowing out to enrich the world around them. We recognize that relationship as a contribution to the furtherance of God's reign on earth. We also affirm our responsibility, as the community in which the relationship has been born, to nurture and support the relationship. To bless a relationship is also to pray for God's continuous presence and protection from forces which threaten it. It is a statement of hope as well as affirmation.

Friends celebrating the blessing of their relationship will want to make clear to each other and to others the commitments upon which their friendship is built, through declarations of hope and promises, but these need not be as far-reaching as a covenant of friendship. It would be entirely appropriate to seek a blessing on a relationship as it moves from one significant stage to another, asking for the continuing presence of God and support from friends. The celebrating of a covenant will usually include a blessing. What will distinguish a blessing from a covenant celebration, apart from the language used, will be the nature of the promises made.

Symbolism

For many people the use of symbols to represent their relationship, remind them of it and what they hope it will be is very important. Although once used as a sign of ownership, rings are now favoured as symbols of people's love and commitment and the exchange of rings as symbolic of mutual giving. Some partners prefer to exchange other gifts. The lighting of candles to symbolize a union can be particularly moving for gay and lesbian people for whom the world can often be a very dark, cold and unwelcoming place. The lighting of candles can also involve relatives and other friends in a pledge to support the relationship in a hostile world. Similarly, sharing a cup of wine, the symbol of goodness and blessing as well as sorrow, can encapsulate the essence of a relationship. The beginning of a new partnership can also be symbolized by the signing of wills, which provide the only legal protection of the rights of one partner if or when the other dies. Some Christians may wish to include a eucharistic celebration in the service, as a way of rooting their commitment in the Christian mission to establish God's commonwealth of justice, peace, freedom and love, of which the eucharist is a foretaste.

Structure

Because celebrations of gay and lesbian partnerships have no legal status there are no structural restraints on those who devise the ceremonies. These ceremonies should be as personal as possible, reflecting the taste and feelings of the partners. This is particularly important as far as the promises are concerned and ideally those making them should write them, taking inspiration from promises made by others. The following is a suggested structure:

> Opening hymn/scriptural sentences
> Introduction
> Prayers
> Declarations of hope
> Charge to witnesses
> Readings and Psalms
> Promises
> Exchange of rings or gifts/candle-ceremony/signing

of will
Blessing
Address/sharing of thoughts
Hymn
Prayers
Eucharist or Symbol of communion
Final Blessing
Hymn and signing of certificate/card

Some people, used to celebrating important occasions in their lives in a church, will want a member of the clergy to lead the service and a church to hold it in. The Lesbian and Gay Christian Movement (LGCM) can provide lists of ministers from various denominations willing to cooperate. Others, perhaps wanting to avoid the impression that they need 'official' ecclesiastical approval for their relationship, may invite a friend to lead the service and opt to hold the service in their home or a hall. Some may wish to ask a large number of people to join their celebration; others who might not be 'out' to their friends or families may opt for a completely private service. The beauty of planning a service of this kind is that there is no set formula, so the service can truly reflect the uniqueness of the relationship.

Since for centuries the only available model for the affirmation of friendship was marriage, it is not surprising that gay and lesbian Christians have taken over some of the symbolism and structure of a wedding ceremony. Some Christians may be concerned that in doing so the participants are trying to claim that the relationship being celebrated is a marriage. I do not think this fear is well grounded. If the liturgy is designed to reflect the nature of the relationship, then it will be obvious to all involved that it is not a wedding. The symbolism associated with marriage will have to be imaginatively reworked to reflect the distinctive-ness of lesbian and gay relationships in general and the uniqueness of the relationship being celebrated in particular. This reworking of traditional symbolism and structures goes on all the time in our society. When I received one of my degrees the ceremony was based upon an ancient ordination rite. The symbolism, words and actions were now in a totally different context. No one participating in or observing the ceremony would have had any doubt that it was a degree ceremony and not an ordination. Similarly, liturgies celebrating lesbian and gay partnerships will quite clearly be just that, although they may use symbolism drawn from the celebrations of heterosexual partnerships.

Historical Perspective

To many it will come as a surprise to learn that public ceremonies affirming the goodness of lesbian and gay relationships have a long history both within and outside of Christianity. Among native American peoples and some African tribes same-sex bonding was common, accepted and celebrated.[3] Same-sex partnerships were legally recognized during the early years of the Roman Empire.[4] It has often been assumed by historians that it was the influence of the Christian faith that led to a change of attitude towards gay and lesbian relationships in the Roman Empire. The growing intolerance resulted in anti-homosexual laws being introduced in the fourth century AD which specifically forbade homosexual 'marriages'. However, the historian John Boswell has questioned the assumption that Christian teaching has always been uniformly against homosexual behaviour. He attributes the intolerance of homosexuality to social rather than religious factors. In an attempt to halt the decline of the Empire the government assumed more and more control over people's lives and any form of social deviance was crushed. Boswell suggests that the arguments against homosexuality now associated with Christianity, for example that sex must be confined to marriage for the sole purpose of procreation, first appeared in these secular, social contexts. In other words, the Christian teaching reflected changes in social attitudes towards homosexuality — it did not inspire those attitudes. Homosexuals were not the only victims of this oppression: Jews, Samaritans, astrologers, actors and others also suffered. During the tenth, eleventh and twelfth centuries, when increased prosperity and urbanization led to greatly increased personal freedom in Western Europe and a glorification of romantic love, there is some evidence that gay and lesbian love was tolerated and celebrated, particularly in monastic writings.

Amongst the wealth of material Boswell unearthed, revealing and celebrating intimate, passionate relationships between same-sex members of religious communities, is a ceremony from the Greek Church of the ninth or tenth century. It is called a ceremony for the making of spiritual brotherhood and Boswell believes it to be 'basically a gay marriage ceremony'. Those wishing to be united were instructed to place their hands on the gospel and hold candles as various prayers were said. I have included some of those prayers from this ceremony in the material that follows.[5] But an even more explicit symbol of love and bonding was also integrated into the ceremony:

The rubric for this ceremony specifies that during much of the ceremony the two parties hold over each other's head the *stephaneis gamou*, that is, the crowns of marriage, which still today in the Orthodox church people who are being married hold over their heads. This renders the ceremony even more electrifying as an archetype of same-sex love in a most decidedly Christian context.[6]

With the thirteenth century came another age of rigid social control and the scapegoating of minorities. Once again Church teaching reflected social opinion. Christian tolerance and celebration of same-sex love such as Boswell discovered in early medieval times has never returned. But it is important for the whole Church to realize that those gay and lesbian Christians who now affirm and celebrate the reality of their love for one another in public liturgical ceremonies are not doing so against the unerring tide of Christian tradition. On the contrary, they are reclaiming and continuing an ancient and honourable tradition.

Sentences from Scriptures and Psalms

1.   This is my commandment, that you love one another as I have loved you. No one has greater love than this, to lay down one's life for one's friends.

(John 15.12–13)

2.   What God has made clean, you must not call profane.

(Acts 10.15)

3.   . . . the fruit of the Spirit is love, joy, peace, patience, kindness, generosity, faithfulness, gentleness, and self-control. There is no law against such things.

(Galatians 5.22–3)

4.   How good it is, and how lovely when friends live
      together as one.
      How lovely the home where your presence dwells, God
      of all creation.
      Happy the people you have inspired, who journey
      through life, with you in their heart.

Who have known both sadness and tears, and covered
   them with blessings, like springs of water.
They go from strength to strength, until they appear
   before God in Zion.
For God withholds no good, from those who walk in
   honesty.

(adapted from Psalms 133 and 84)

5. Make a joyful noise to the Lord, all the earth.
    Worship the Lord with gladness;
    come into his presence singing.

    Know that the Lord is God.
    It is he that made us, and we are his;
    we are his people, and the sheep of his pasture.

    Enter his gates with thanksgiving,
    and his courts with praise.
    Give thanks to him, bless his name.

    For the Lord is good;
    his steadfast love endures forever,
    and his faithfulness to all generations.

(Psalm 100)

6. Praise the Lord, all you nations!
    Extol him, all you peoples!
    For great is his steadfast love toward us,
    and the faithfulness of the Lord endures forever.
    Praise the Lord.

(Psalm 117)

7. We praise you dear God in your holy city,
    we renew our vows in the holy places.
    For you meet us in the depth of our being,

when we come to confess all that is true of us.
When our misdeeds haunt us with their power,
your generous love sweeps them aside.

Let the people praise you, O God: let all creation praise you.

Blessed are those whom you choose as your friends,
who lodge with you in your house.
You empower them with talents and gifts,
you crown them with an abundance of blessings.

Let the people praise you, O God: let all creation praise you.

In dread deeds you will deliver us,
O God of our salvation,
for you are the hope of the ends of the earth,
and of the distant seas.

Let the people praise you, O God: let all creation praise you.

By your strength you make the mountains rise,
by your power you gouge the valleys deep.
You still the raging of the seas,
the roaring of the waves,
and the tumult of the peoples.

Let the people praise you, O God: let all creation praise you.

Those who dwell at the ends of the earth
are held in awe at your wonders:
the dawn and the evening sing your praise.

Let the people praise you, O God: let all creation praise you.

You tend the earth and you water it,
you make it rich and fertile.
Your clouds are full of water,

they provide rain for the swelling grain.

Let the people praise you, O God: let all creation praise you.

You drench the furrows,
you level the ridges between,
you soften the soil with showers
and bless its early growth.
You refresh hearts withered and dry,
you bring to life the land parched with drought.

Let the people praise you, O God: let all creation praise you.

You crown our years with good gifts,
the fruit trees drip with abundance.
The alpine pastures shimmer with green,
the hills are wreathed with dancing clouds.
The meadows are clothed with sheep,
and the valleys mantled with corn.

Let the people praise you, O God: let all creation praise you.

(version of Psalm 65 by Jim Cotter)

Introductions

1. In the presence of God we have come together to witness the celebration and blessing of the loving union which exists between N and N. They have come to affirm and deepen their love and commitment to each other and to ask God's blessing as they offer their life together to him.

In this service we remind ourselves of our human vocation which is to love God and to love our neighbour. God has created us that we might grow in love. We respond to his love in many ways, always remembering that the marks of true love are shown to us in Jesus Christ: self-sacrifice, commitment, respect, a mutual giving and receiving, and a determination to avoid all force, triviality or exploitation.

From the earliest times men and women have made solemn vows in the sight of God and before witnesses. The stories of David and Jonathan and Ruth and Naomi remind us of two such vows, made before God, and calling on God to witness and bless the love they swore to each other for ever.

We are here today so that N and N may bear witness to their love for each other, and so that we may share in their happiness and joy. We have come to witness this exchange of promises because we believe that God, who is love and truth, sees into all our hearts, and longs to bless us, and to bless N and N, recognizing their love and accepting the offering they are making.

(Jim Cotter)

2.   We have come here this day to this holy place to recognize and honour a holy relationship – the love of N and N for each other and their wish to make life-long commitments to one another which others will honour and respect.

(Andrew Hill)

3.   Welcome to this service celebrating and affirming the loving relationship between N and N. You are all part of the service, not an audience. Your interest, your love and prayers will mean much to both of them.

It is written that the greatest of all things, the most wonderful experience in the world, is love. N and N, into your lives has entered a deep and lasting love and you have asked this church and its ministry to help you celebrate and affirm that love.

We would call your love partnership a holy union, for where there is love, God is there also.

Ever since there have been human beings, there have been some of us who have shared the deepest expressions of love with someone of the same sex. Many Christians have grown to recognize the validity of that special way of loving and they work, with many others, to overcome the prejudice about it in society.

N and N, you have done us the honour of inviting us to witness your commitment to each other.

(Dudley Cave)

4.   We are here today so that N and N may bear witness to their love for each other, and so that we may share in their happiness and joy. We have come to witness this exchange of promises because we believe that God, who is love and truth, sees into all our hearts, and longs to bless us, and to bless N and N, recognizing their love and accepting the offering they are making, and to ask God's blessing as they offer their life to him.

(Hazel Barkham)

5.   *Partner A*: We stand here today in the presence of people from so many parts of our journeys. You are the people who have been family for us. We rejoice that you have come to witness our beginning, our new family.

Partner B: We have brought this community of friends and colleagues together to celebrate the beginning of a new part of our journey. We are here to make a covenant together.

We rejoice to be part of this celebration. We have loved and valued you separately. We will continue to love and value you in relationship.

(Phyllis Athey and Mary Jo Osterman)

Prayers

1. Father of all mercies and giver of all grace, we commend to you these your servants, N and N, who desire your help and guidance for the new life which they begin together this day. Grant them the grace of love and forbearance; grant them your pure and peaceable wisdom to enlighten them in all perplexities, and the power of your Holy Spirit in their hearts to keep constant their trust in you and one another; through Jesus Christ our Lord.

(Jim Cotter)

2. Lord, look upon N and N, who are choosing to be life companions in your sight. You who are greater than our hearts, you know what this has demanded of them, of time, of suffering, to accept and love themselves as they are. You have made yourself known to them as a God who prefers mercy to sacrifices, humility to perfection, the individual to the law. They have in you not a judge or enemy but an exacting and faithful friend who commits himself/ herself in our hearts, and our weaknesses, to trace in them a path of life, of freedom, of love and of faithfulness. May they find peace in their hearts in the certainty that you love them, that you accompany them in today's decision. May they confirm their commitment and grow in faith with those who are united with us in this act of prayer.

(anonymous)

3. God of all, source and goal of community, whose will is that all your people enjoy fullness of life, may we be builders of community, caring for your good earth here and worldwide, that we may delight in diversity and choose solidarity, for you are in community with us our God for ever.

(anonymous)

4.   O God, creator and lover of the world, we offer to you our lives, our words and deeds, our hopes and fears, and our love for each other. Accept us as we are. Make us what we shall be. And by the power of your spirit enable us to be a sign of your presence in the world; through Jesus Christ our Lord.

(Jim Cotter)

5.   We believe that by our love we bear witness to the union of Christ and his Church. We believe that we are meant to be for each other a sign of Christ's love. We believe that we are called to bring each other to God. We believe that we are called to build up the family of God.

(Jim Cotter)

6.   Conscious of the many meanings of this hour and overjoyed at its promises, we pray that the spirit of trust, understanding and love may be with N and N in all the years that lie ahead. Whatever the trials and testings that may come, may they trust each other wholly, for without such faith a formal affirmation of their commitment is a mockery. May they understand each other for, without understanding, there is neither acceptance nor forgiveness. As they build their home together may it be bright with the laughter of many friends, may it be a haven from the tensions of our times and a source of strength and security and, in all the world, may it be the one place they most want to be. May the years deal gently with them. Walking together may they find far more in life than either would have found alone. And even more fully may they come to know the great truths: that caring is sharing and living is giving.

(Dudley Cave)

7.   We pray that there may be concord and creativity as well as love and laughter in N and N's life together. When there is pain, may there be peace which passes not away.

We pray for the joy they will share with other people, and for their home, may it be a temple for that which is beautiful, good and true. As they share the experience of life, so may their hearts, minds and souls be knit ever closer together. And yet may their bonds of sympathy strengthen their separate personalities.

We pray for courage for them when the road is rough, and for humility for them when fortune favours them. May they carry the past gracefully with them and, with equal measure of hope, face the future unafraid.

(Dudley Cave)

8.   For the servants of God who have come to be blessed in this church, and for their love,

we pray to the Lord;

that the knowledge of the apostolic unity of the spirit might be given to them,

we pray to the Lord;

that they may be vouchsafed unashamed fidelity, faithfulness and unfeigned love,

we pray to the Lord;

that they may be made worthy to glory in the Holy Cross,

we pray to the Lord;

that they and we may be saved from every tribulation, trouble and danger,

we pray to the Lord.

(anonymous, ninth or tenth century AD)

9.   O Lord, our God, who hast bestowed all things on us for salvation and hast commended us to love one another and to bear with another's weaknesses, you yourself who are now a lover of humankind, to these your servants who love each other in the love of the spirit, and have come into your holy temple to be blessed by you, grant unashamed devotion and unfeigned love.

And as you gave to your holy disciples your peace, grant also to these all things needed for salvation and eternal life, which we pray God, to you who are lover of humankind, and we render glory to you, to the Father, the Son and the Holy Spirit.

(anonymous, ninth or tenth century AD)

10.   O Lord, our God, ruler of all, you make heaven and earth and the sea and human beings in your image and likeness, and you thought well of it when your holy martyrs Sergius and Bacchus were joined together, not bound by the law of nature, but by the example of the faithfulness of the Holy Spirit; do you, O Lord, send down your Holy Spirit on these your children, who have come into this temple to be blessed. Grant them unashamed fidelity and honest love, and may they be unhated and not a cause of scandal all the days of their lives, following the example of your immaculate mother and all the saints. For yours is the kingdom and the power and glory. Praise to the Father and to the Son and to the Holy Spirit, glory now and forever, world without end.

(anonymous, ninth or tenth century AD)

11.   O Holy Spirit who is known to us as love, we pray that these two people may keep the covenant which they have made. May they find much happiness, and fulfilment in their lives together, marked by a sense of personal freedom as well as mutual responsibility. May they find in each other companionship

as well as love, understanding as well as compassion, challenge as well as agreement. Shall we spend a few moments in quietness together, each with our own thoughts and wishes ... It is our great adventure in faith, our life-long giving and receiving of the unending blessings of life.

(Ann Peart)

Declarations and Questions of Hope

1.   We have gathered together today to acknowledge the love which has brought N and N together as being from God and to ask God's blessing upon them as they live together in company with each other. We also seek to give them support as their friends and as members of the Body of Christ, the Church, and to strive for their good now in our prayers and in our future care and concern.

Each friend repeats the following: In the presence of God and God's people, I, N, declare my love for you, N, and seek God's blessing on our friendship. I will continue to love you, care for you, and consider you before my own needs, in good times and through periods of difficulty. I will rejoice when you are happy and grieve when you suffer. I will share your interests and hopes for the future. I will try to understand you even when I do not agree with you. I will help you to be your true self – the person God wishes you to be. In all this I ask God's help, now and in the days to come. In the name of Jesus Christ. Amen.

(Hazel Barkham)

2.   N and N, you are about to make a solemn promise. Do you believe God has called you to live together in love?

We do believe.

Do you promise to be loyal to each other, never allowing any other relationship to come before the one you are now to affirm?

We do promise.

Will you give yourselves wholeheartedly and without reserve?

We will.

Will you, under God, recognize each other's freedom to grow as individuals and allow each other time and space to do so?

We will.

Will you do all in your power to make your life together a witness to the love of God in the world?

We will.

To each partner in turn: N, will you give yourself wholly to N, sharing your love and your life, your wholeness and your brokenness, your joys and sorrows, your health and sickness, your riches and poverty, your success and failure?

I will.

(Jim Cotter)

3.   Today we pledge ourselves to a commitment in love. Our commitment to each other comes from a belief that God is with us. In our union we would seek to offer companionship to each other in every area of our life together. We would seek to bear fruit through our relationship, in the way it touches our family, our friends and those around us.

(anonymous)

4.   *To each partner in turn*: Will you, N, unite your life with N's life. Will you honour him/her, support him/her, cherish him/her and stand with him/her all your days?

I will.

Trials will come, and tests, for there is much in this world of ours that would long to pull you apart. Do you bring strength and vision to your relationship, courage and understanding?

We do.

Joys will come, graces and blessings will warm your souls and give you wonder. Do you bring thanksgiving and rejoicing to this relationship, laughter and abandon?

We do.

(Terry Kime and Sally Meiser)

Charges to Witnesses

1.   Will you, the chosen witnesses this day of N and N, do all in your power to support and strengthen them in the days ahead?

We will.

(Jim Cotter)

2.   N and N, you have proclaimed your commitment in this holy place before your community of friends. I invite everyone to join me in the confirmation of this union.

In the presence of this good company, by the power of your

**love, because you have exchanged vows of commitment, we
recognize you as united.**

(Terry Kime and Sally Meiser)

3.   The ceremony in which we are all now participating is a bold,
even revolutionary act. As you all know, many in our society do
not yet recognize the validity and worth of the relationship we
today celebrate and affirm; indeed, many are openly hostile to
two persons of the same gender who decide to commit their lives
to one another. We pray that someday men who love men and
women who love women will no longer feel the scorn of some.
But in the meantime, we can express the joy and approval we feel
for N and N as they give public recognition to the love they feel
for each other, and the commitment they freely make to one
another this day. Let me therefore ask those of you who have
gathered here today this: do you who know and care for N and N
give them your blessings now as they enter into this new
relationship, and do you promise to give them your deepest love,
understanding, and support during both good times and bad?

We do.

(Scott W. Alexander)

Promises

1.   I, N, take you, N, to be my beloved partner, to love and to
cherish all my days.

(Terry Kime and Sally Meiser)

2.   In the presence of God and God's people, I, N, declare my
love for you, N, and seek God's blessing on our friendship. I will

continue to love you, care for you, and consider you before my own needs, in good times and through periods of difficulty; I will rejoice when you are happy and grieve when you suffer; I will share your interests and hopes for the future; I will try to understand you even when I do not agree with you; I will help you to be your true self – the person God wishes you to be. In all this I ask God's help, now and in the days to come. In the name of Jesus Christ. Amen.

(Hazel Barkham)

3.   Will you, N, take N to be your life-long companion, lover and friend? Will you spend your lives together, seeking to fulfil each other's needs, growing together that you may share your strengths and bear each other's weaknesses? Do you promise to love, honour and cherish him/her, to dwell together in harmony and love as long as you both shall live?

Partners in turn: I do.

(Neil Thomas)

4.   In the Mystery of Divine Love
        you have been given to me, N,
        and in my own free will and destiny.
        I embrace you,
        choosing and being chosen
        to share with you my being and becoming.
        And with and in that Love,
        I promise to be for you
        and for your well-being for ever,
        to honour you as a dwelling place of God,
        and to be loyal to you
        and full of faith in you,
        our life-day long.

(Jim Cotter)

5. I take you, N, to be my partner and I promise you these
    things:
    I will be faithful to you and honest with you.
    I will respect you, trust you, help you, listen to you, and
        care for you.
    I will share my life with you in plenty and in want.
    I will forgive you as we have been forgiven, and I will
        try with you to better understand ourselves, the
        world, and God
    so that together we may serve God and others forever.

    (Rosemary Radford Ruether)

6. I, N, take you, N, to be no other than yourself. Loving what I
    know of you, trusting what I don't yet know, with respect to your
    integrity and faith in your love for me, through our years together,
    and in all that life may bring us, I accept you as my partner in life.

    (F. Jay Deacon)

Exchange of Rings or Gifts

1. Lord, bless these rings/gifts which we bless in your name:
    grant that they who wear them may always have a deep faith in
    each other. May they do your will, and live together in peace
    and love, sharing their joys and their fears, and each with
    patience and trust giving the other room to grow in freedom and
    in truth; through Jesus Christ our Lord.

Partners in turn: This ring/gift is a sign of all that I am and all that
I have. Receive and treasure it as a token and pledge of the love

that I have for you; and wear/carry it as a protection whenever we are separated.

(Jim Cotter)

2. This simple gold band is a symbol of God's eternal love and of the love and unity of the one who wears it.

Partners in turn: N, in accepting this ring I join my life with yours.

(Neil Thomas)

3. *Partners in turn*: N, I give you this ring so that you may choose to wear it and in so doing be reminded and re-experience my deep love and regard for you and my wish that you may have a long life and a beautifully rich and creative one.

N, I will wear this love gift with honour and joy as a sign to others that I am committed to our union.

(Marion Hansell and Barbara Hicks)

4. The circle is a symbol of the sun and of the earth and the universe. It is a symbol of wholeness and of perfection and of peace. The ring is a symbol of unity into which your two lives are now joined in an unbroken circle, in which, wherever you go, you will return to one another. As you place your rings on each other's fingers say, 'I give you this ring as a symbol of our union and our love.'

(Judith Meyer)

Blessings

1. Spirit of God, teaching us through the Lord Jesus that love is the fulfilling of the law, help N and N to persevere in love, to

grow in mutual understanding, and to deepen their trust in each other, that in wisdom, patience and courage, their love may be a source of happiness and their home a place of peace to all with whom they share it. God the Father, God the Son and God the Holy Spirit, bless, preserve and keep you, the Lord make his face to shine upon you and be gracious to you, guide you in truth and peace, make you strong in love and faith, that you may so grow together in this life that your love may be taken up even beyond death itself, and be fulfilled in eternity.

(Jim Cotter)

2.   Blessed are you, O God, the ruler of the universe, who creates the fruit of the vine.

Blessed are you, O God, the ruler of the universe, who was created according to his desire.

Blessed are you, O God, the ruler of the universe who has created everything for his glory.

Blessed are you, O God, the ruler of the universe, who forms all human beings.

Blessed are you, O God, the ruler of the universe, who formed us in his image, that we might help each other and lead each other into goodness.

Blessed are you, God, who sets eternal life within us.

Blessed are you, O God, the ruler of the universe, who created joy and happiness, love and companionship, and friendship. May these companions in love bring joy to each other, rejoice in the house of Israel, and give comfort to all. Blessed are you, God, who is good and does good.

Blessed are you, O God, the ruler of the universe, who has kept us alive, and supported us, and brought us to this season.

May God bless you and keep you.

May God's face enlighten you, and be kind to you.
May God turn his face towards you and give you peace.

(Malcolm Johnson)

3.   May these two people find a communion of ideal being and perfect grace. May their love reach the level of every day's quiet need. By sun and by candlelight may they love freely as people strive for right; may they love purely; may they find the strength to meet the adversities, tolerance for the prejudice, reverence for the beauties, respect for the truths and faith for the uncertainties which will come their way. Amen.

(Dudley Cave)

4.   May the Lord protect and defend you.
May he always shield you from shame.
May you come to be in paradise a shining name.
May you be like Ruth and Naomi/David and Jonathan.
May you be deserving of praise.
Strengthen them, O Lord, and keep them from all danger-
ous ways.
May God bless you and grant you long life.
May God make you good partners for life.
May the Lord protect and defend you.
May the Lord preserve you from pain.
Favour them, O Lord, with happiness and peace.
O, hear our Sabbath prayer. Amen.

(Marion Hansell and Barbara Hicks)

5.   Blessed are those who come together in God's name. We bless you from his house. And may the Eternal, whose greatness transcends us, yet sets within us the power of his friendship and love, bless these friends, who are gathered here.

(Malcolm Johnson)

6.   O Lord our God, dwelling in heaven but looking down on that which is below, you who for the salvation of the human race sent your only begotten son, Jesus, and took Peter and Paul and made them brothers by consecration, make also these your servants N and N like those two apostles. Keep them blameless all the days of their lives. Lord of all and maker of humankind in your image and likeness, you who gave humankind eternal life, consider as worthy to become brothers these two, not joined by nature but by the holy attraction of fidelity and of the mind, just as he unified Sergius and Bacchus, Cosmas and Damien, and Cyrus and John. Bless also these your servants N and N not joined by nature but by means of love. Give them love toward each other, and may their union remain without hatred or scandal all the days of their lives through the power of your most Holy Spirit.

(anonymous, ninth or tenth century AD)

Candle-lighting Ceremonies

1.   We live in many darknesses. We are often uncertain. We are sometimes afraid. In the darkness, we light a candle of hope.

A candle is lit.

We all have sorrows. We have known pain. Each of us carries special regrets. In our pain we light a candle of forgiveness.

A candle is lit.

We are sometimes lonely, and the world seems cold and hard. In our loneliness, we light a candle of warmth.

A candle is lit.

We have our joys, our times of happiness. Each of us receives gifts. In our gratification we light a candle of thanks.

A candle is lit.

We have known awe, wonder, mystery, glimmerings of perfection in our imperfect world. In our wonder we light a candle of praise.

A candle is lit.

We bring together many uncertainties, many sorrows, many joys, much wonder. We bring together many candles, many lights.

May our separate lights become one flame, that together we may be nourished by its glow.

(Bruce Marshall)

2.   *On the altar, or in the centre of the gathering, are placed three candles. At the beginning of the service the couple each light one of the outer candles. After the formal blessing of their relationship they take each of the lighted candles and light the central candle. They then extinguish the two other candles. This symbolizes their union.*

(Neil Thomas)

3.   *Each partner lights a candle and the couple say together:* As we bring together the two candles of our lives up until this moment, we ask that our bond be as vibrant and as illuminating as this new flame, that it continually be renewed by the strengths of our individual selves, and that, like this powerful flame, our life together may radiate light and warmth. Holy One of Blessing, your presence fills creation forming the lights of fire.

(Rosanne Leipzig and Judy Mable)

Symbols of Communion

1. In this flowering time of women in the world, at this ceremony of union for N and N, we come together in bondedness expressed in these symbols of life – bread and wine.

All extend their hands over the bread and wine.

We bless this bread, nurturing Creator, to celebrate your being our God and our being your bread. May we be nurturers in your world and help it to grow in wholeness.

We bless this wine, nurturing Creator, that we might become zest for your universe, spark for your tired ones, energy for one another.

(Rose Tillemans)

2. *Partner A*: Let us drink from one cup to remember the joys and sorrows we shall share, which are given us to grow together.

Partner B extends his/her hand over the wine and says: Blessed are you, the eternal our God, who creates the fruit of the vine.

The leader gives each of them the cup of wine.

Partner B: Let us eat this bread to remember our daily bread, and our daily life together. May God hallow the small and ordinary things of life through his blessing.

Partner A extends his/her hand over the bread and says: Blessed are you, the eternal our God, who brings forth bread from the earth.

The leader gives each of them the bread.

(Malcolm Johnson)

3.   This communion is our gift to the community. It symbolizes connections of the past with the present and the present with the future. We invite the congregation to join in a circle for the rite of connection, the prayer circle, and the communion. It is an open circle to which all are invited.

Partner A: This chalice of water holds the tears of the oppressed ones who have gone before us. I draw the sign of the tear on your face.

The cup is passed from one person to the next with each marking a sign of a tear on the next person's cheek.

Partner B: This basket of raisins is the dried-up dreams of the generations who were not free. It symbolizes the work and the hopes we have lost.

The raisins are passed and shared.

Partner A: This basket of fresh cool grapes symbolizes our work, our dreams and our hopes; it is the fruit of the New Earth.

Partner B: This loaf of bread made with raisins is the new wheat and the old raisins mixed together to feed us for the journey. We claim the past, we move into the future. We offer this bread for communion.

The grapes and bread are passed and shared.

(Phyllis Athey and Mary Jo Osterman)

4.   This cup of wine is symbolic of the cup of life. As you share this one cup of wine, may life be that much sweeter because you share it, and if there is any bitterness within your lives together, may the bitterness be that much less bitter also because you share. Let us say together:

Blessed are you, Lord our God, ruler of the universe, creator of the fruit of the vine.

(Rosanne Leipzig and Judy Mable)

5.   'Love one another, but make not a bond of love: let it rather be a moving sea between the shores of your souls. Fill each other's cup but drink not from one cup.' Will you now each drink to one another, filling each other's cup, as Gibran says, but drinking from your own. Remember that what matters most is not the cup, but the wine of life within it. You can enrich each other's lives, but you must drink from your own.

Each fills the other's cup from a common container, then each drinks from his/her own. If it is practical, wine can then be poured for the others present, who hold it as the following is said:

As N and N have asked us to share their joy, they are also asking us to share the responsibility of a loving community. As they must stand apart from each other while sharing their lives, so we must stand apart from them. Let us not forget that a partnership is a private matter between two independent human beings — a relationship upon which no one should presume to intrude without invitation. Will you stand by them, hands open in friendship and support, caring but not crowding, listening when asked but not directing or giving unwanted advice? Will you, as a community, share this responsibility?

We will.

All drink.

(F. Jay Deacon)

Final Blessings

1. May all the blessings of God rest upon you today and
always. Go in peace and celebrate your life. Know that God is
with you. Amen.

(Metropolitan Community Church)

2. We have claimed past tears and lost dreams. We have
entered into a new covenant and tasted its goodness. We now
go forward on the journey. Amen.

(Phyllis Athey and Mary Jo Osterman)

3.   Above you are the stars
        Below you are the stones,
        As time does pass
        Remember . . .
        Like a star should your love be constant.
        Like a stone should your love be firm.
        Be close, yet not too close.
        Possess one another, yet be understanding.
        Have patience each with the other
        For storms will come, but they will go quickly.
        Be free in giving of affection and warmth.
        Make love often, and be sensuous to one another.
        Have no fear, and let not the ways or words
        Of the unenlightened give you unease.
        For the spirit is with you.
        Now and always.

(F. Jay Deacon)

4. May the love in your hearts give you joy. May the greatness
of life bring you peace. And may your days be good, and your
lives be long upon the earth. So be it.

(F. Jay Deacon)

Certificates of Contract

1.   On the ... day of ... [month] ... [year], the companions N and N proposed to each other that they enter into a covenant of friendship and loyalty, to honour each other, and the community and to bring glory to the Holy One who sows the seed of Eve and salvation in every person and nurtures it within them.

And N said I shall ... [signature of partner 1]
and N replied to this and said I shall ... [signature of partner 2]

And they accepted each other's promises and entered into this covenant of friendship and loyalty, of honesty and trust. And they agreed to hallow their home for their own good, and for the good of the community, and for the glory of the Holy One, blessed be his name.

The covenant was duly signed and witnessed in our presence.
... day of ... [month] ... [year]
Signature of witnesses: ...

                                        (Malcolm Johnson)

2.   We N and N have chosen to share our lives. Today, at a service of celebration, we affirmed our promises to love each other, to do all we can for the other's well-being and to be loyal to each other before all others.

As tokens of our love we have exchanged rings, which we see as symbols of the promises we have made here today.

Signed: ... [signature of partner 1]
        ... [signature of partner 2]

Witnessed by: . . . [signatures of witnesses]

Date: . . .

(Ann Peart)

Readings

1.   Ruth said [to Naomi]:
     Do not press me to leave you
     or to turn back from following you!
     Where you go, I will go;
     Where you lodge, I will lodge;
     your people shall be my people,
     and your God my God.
     Where you die, I will die –
     there will I be buried.
     May the Lord do thus and so to me,
     and more as well,
     if even death parts me from you!

(Ruth 1.16–17)

2.   . . . the soul of Jonathan was bound to the soul of David, and
     Jonathan loved him as his own soul . . . Then Jonathan made a
     covenant with David, because he loved him as his own soul . . .
     Jonathan made a covenant with the house of David, saying, 'May
     the Lord seek out the enemies of David.' Jonathan made David
     swear again by his love for him; for he loved him as he loved his
     own life . . . Then Jonathan said to David, 'Go in peace, since
     both of us have sworn in the name of the Lord, saying, "The
     Lord shall be between me and you, and between my descendants
     and your descendants, forever."'

(1 Samuel 18.1*b*, 3 and 20.16–17, 42*a*)

3.   Two are better than one, because they have a good reward for their toil. For if they fall, one will lift up the other; but woe to one who is alone and falls and does not have another to help. Again, if two lie together, they keep warm; but how can one keep warm alone? And though one might prevail against another, two will withstand one. A threefold cord is not quickly broken.

(Ecclesiastes 4.9–12)

4.   The voice of my beloved!
     Look, he comes,
     leaping upon the mountains,
     bounding over the hills.
     My beloved is like a gazelle
     or a young stag.
     Look, there he stands
     behind our wall,
     gazing in at the windows,
     looking through the lattice.
     My beloved speaks and says to me:
     'Arise, my love, my fair one,
     and come away;
     for now the winter is past,
     the rain is over and gone.
     The flowers appear on the earth;
     the time of singing has come,
     and the voice of the turtledove is heard in our land.
     The fig tree puts forth its figs,
     and the vines are in blossom;
     they give forth fragrance.
     Arise, my love, my fair one,
     and come away.'

(Song of Solomon 2.8–13)

5.   Set me as a seal upon your heart,
      as a seal upon your arm;
      for love is strong as death,
      passion fierce as the grave.
      Its flashes are flashes of fire, a raging flame.
      Many waters cannot quench love,
      neither can floods drown it.
      If one offered for love
      all the wealth of his house,
      it would be utterly scorned.

                              (Song of Solomon 8.6–7)

6.   Then he looked up at his disciples and said:
      Blessed are you who are poor,
      for yours is the kingdom of God.
      Blessed are you who are hungry now,
      for you will be filled.
      Blessed are you who weep now,
      for you will laugh.

   Blessed are you when people hate you, and when they exclude
you, revile you, and defame you on account of the Son of Man.
Rejoice in that day and leap for joy, for surely your reward
is great in heaven; for that it is what their ancestors did to the
prophets.

                              (Luke 6.20–3)

7.   Let love be genuine; hate what is evil, hold fast to what is
good; love one another with mutual affection; outdo one another
in showing honour. Do not lag in zeal, be ardent in spirit, serve
the Lord. Rejoice in hope, be patient in suffering, persevere in
prayer. Contribute to the needs of the saints; extend hospitality
to strangers.

Bless those who persecute you; bless and do not curse them. Rejoice with those who rejoice, weep with those who weep. Live in harmony with one another; do not be haughty, but associate with the lowly; do not claim to be wiser than you are. Do not repay anyone evil for evil, but take thought for what is noble in the sight of all. If it is possible, as far as it depends on you, live peaceably with all. Beloved, never avenge yourselves, but leave room for the wrath of God; for it is written, 'Vengeance is mine, I will repay, says the Lord.' No, 'if your enemies are hungry, feed them; if they are thirsty, give them something to drink; for by doing this you will heap burning coals on their heads'. Do not be overcome by evil, but overcome evil with good.

(Romans 12.9–21)

8.   If I speak in the tongues of mortals and of angels, but do not have love, I am a noisy gong or a clanging cymbal. And if I have prophetic powers, and understand all mysteries and all knowledge, and if I have all faith, so as to remove mountains, but do not have love, I am nothing. If I give away all my possessions, and if I hand over my body so that I may boast, but do not have love, I gain nothing.

Love is patient; love is kind; love is not envious or boastful or arrogant or rude. It does not insist on its own way; it is not irritable or resentful; it does not rejoice in wrong-doing, but rejoices in the truth. It bears all things, believes all things, hopes all things, endures all things.

Love never ends. But as for prophecies, they will come to an end; as for tongues, they will cease; as for knowledge, it will come to an end. For we know only in part, and we prophesy only in part; but when the complete comes, the partial will come to an end. When I was a child, I spoke like a child, I thought like a child, I reasoned like a child; when I became an adult, I put an

end to childish ways. For now we see in a mirror, dimly, but then
we will see face to face. Now I know only in part; then I will
know fully, even as I have been fully known. And now faith,
hope, and love abide, these three; and the greatest of these is
love.

(1 Corinthians 13)

9.   Beloved, let us love one another, because love is from God;
everyone who loves is born of God and knows God. Whoever
does not love does not know God, for God is love. God's love
was revealed among us in this way: God sent his only Son into
the world so that we might live through him. In this is love, not
that we loved God but that he loved us and sent his Son to be
the atoning sacrifice for our sins. Beloved, since God loved us so
much, we also ought to love one another. No one has ever seen
God; if we love one another, God lives in us, and his love is
perfected in us.

(1 John 4.7–12)

10.   Now you will feel no rain, for each of you will be shelter
         for the other.
      Now you will feel no cold, for each of you will be
         warmth to the other.
      Now there is no more loneliness.
      Now you are two persons, but there is only one life
         before you.
      Go now to your dwelling to enter into the days of your
         life together.
      And may your days be good and long upon the earth.

(from a native American ceremony)

11.   It is not enough to love passionately; you must also love

well. A passionate love is good, doubtless, but a beautiful love is better. May you have as much strength as gentleness; may it lack nothing, not even forbearance, and let even a little compassion be mingled with it ... You are human, and because of this capable of much suffering. If then something of compassion does not enter into the feelings you have one for the other, these feelings will not always befit all the circumstances of your life together; they will be like festive robes that will not shield you from wind and rain. We love truly only those we love even in their weakness and their poverty. To forbear, to forgive, to console, that alone is the science of love.

(Anatole France)

12. It is for the union of you and me
     that there is light in the sky.
     It is for the union of you and me
     that the earth is decked in dusky green.
     It is for the union of you and me
     that the night sits motionless with the world in her arms;
     dawn appears opening the eastern door
     with sweet murmurs in her voice.

     The boat of hope sails along the currents of
     eternity towards that union,
     flowers of the ages are being gathered together
     for its welcoming ritual.

     It is for the union of you and me
     that this heart of mine, in the garb of a bride,
     has proceeded from birth to birth
     upon the surface of this ever-turning world
     to choose the beloved.

(Rabindranath Tagore)

13.   In living the youness of you,
      be prepared to go outside the gate in giving all.
      But first, keep asking,
      What is your deepest desire now?
      In desiring to give yourself utterly,
      do not do so prematurely,
      before you have become the fullest self
      that it is possible for you to become.
      There are many lesser desirings and givings
      that must have their place.
      Not least among these are affection, companionship,
      falling asleep in the arms of those who love you,
      the making of love.
      And when such lesser desires are being fulfilled,
      rejoice in what is, however incomplete.
      If you expect all,
      you will be worshipping an idol,
      not enjoying life with another human being.

                                                    (Jim Cotter)

14.   Let your love be exclusive, but not exclusive:
      special, but not excluding.
      You do not matter to each other more than anything
         else
      or more than anyone else in the world.
      But you matter to each other in a unique way
      that no one can replace,
      and that matters to each of you very much indeed.

                                                    (Jim Cotter)

15.   Truthful love counts for everything. For me, to be in love is
to be in God who is within every person he created and knows
to be good. For me the mystery of God is the mystery of love

and that love never ever casts out love. Similarly, I believe that love is able to understand and to cope with all our unloving ways to which we are all vulnerable.

(Bill Kirkpatrick)

16.   To say I love you is to say that you are not mine, but rather your own.

To love you is to advocate your rights, your space, your self, and to struggle with you, rather than against you, in our learning to claim our power in the world.

To love you is to make love to you, and with you, whether in an exchange of glances heavy with existence, in the passing of a peace we mean, in common work or play, in our struggle for social justice, or in the ecstasy and tenderness of intimate embrace that we believe is just and right for us – and for others in the world.

To love you is to be pushed by a power/God both terrifying and comforting, to touch and be touched by you. To love you is to sing with you, cry with you, pray with you, and act with you to re-create the world.

To say 'I love you' means – let the revolution begin!

(Carter Heyward)

17.   Keep your passion alive –
it will warm you when the
world around you grows cold.
It will not allow comfortable
familiarity to rob you of that
special glow that comes with
loving deeply. It can lift
you over stone walls of anger

and carry you across vast
deserts of alienation. But its
greatest gift is that of touch —
for passion cannot dwell in
solitude — it thrives best in
loving embrace. So keep your
passion alive — hold one
another as a tree holds the
Earth and your love will
bear the fruit of many,
many seasons!

(Atimah)

18. From every human being there rises
a light that reaches straight to heaven.
And when two souls that are destined to be together
find each other, their streams of light flow together,
and a single brighter light goes forth from their united
being.

(Baal Shem Tov)

19. Love is a sacred mystery.
To those who love, it remains forever wordless;
But to those who do not love, it may be but a heartless
jest.
Love is a gracious host to his guests though to the
unbidden his house is a mirage and a mockery.
Love is a night where candles burn in space,
Love is a dream beyond our reaching;
Love is a noon where all shepherds are at peace and
happy that their flocks are grazing;
Love is an eventide and a stillness, and a homecoming;
Love is a sleep and a dream.

When love becomes vast love becomes wordless.
And when memory is overladen it seeks the silent deep.

(Kahlil Gibran)

20. Love is a mighty power, a great and complete good; love alone lightens every heavy burden, and makes the rough places smooth. It bears every hardship as though it were nothing, and renders all bitterness sweet and acceptable . . . Love aspires to high things, and is held back by nothing base. Love longs to be free, a stranger to every worldly desire, lest its inner vision become dimmed, and lest worldly self-interest hinder it or ill-fortune cast it down. Nothing is sweeter than love, nothing stronger, nothing higher, nothing wider, nothing more pleasant, nothing fuller or better in heaven or earth; for love is born of God, and can rest only in God, above all created things.

Love flies, runs, and leaps for joy; it is free and unrestrained. Love gives all for all, resting in One who is highest above all things, from whom every good flows and proceeds. Love does not regard the gifts, but turns to the Giver of all good gifts. Love knows no limits, but ardently transcends all bounds. Love feels no burden, takes no account of toil, attempts things beyond its strength; love sees nothing as impossible, for it feels able to achieve all things. Love therefore does great things; it is strange and effective; while he who lacks love faints and falls.

Love is watchful, and while resting, never sleeps; weary, it is never exhausted; imprisoned, it is never in bonds; alarmed, it is never afraid; like a living flame and a burning torch, it surges upward and surely surmounts every obstacle.

(Thomas à Kempis)

The following poems are also offered as suggested readings:

W. H. Auden, 'Lay Your Sleeping Head, My Love'; Elizabeth Barrett Browning, 'Sonnets from the Portuguese XLIII'; e. e. cummings,

'somewhere i have never travelled'; Kahlil Gibran, *The Prophet*, pp.
12–17, 78–80; George Herbert, 'Love'; Adrienne Rich, *Twenty-One
Love Poems*; Dante Gabriel Rossetti, 'Sudden Light'; Philip Sidney,
'My True Love Hath My Heart'; William Shakespeare, Sonnet CXI;
Stephen Spender, 'Earth-Treading Stars that Made Dark Heaven
Light'; Walt Whitman, Selections from *Leaves of Grass*; John Wilmot,
Earl of Rochester, 'A Song of a Young Lady to her Ancient Lover';
Walter Tubbs, 'Beyond Pearls'; Fyodor Tyutchev, 'Last Love'; and
Frank Yerby, 'You are a Part of Me'.

Other recommended sources for readings are the Oxford Book of
Friendship, ed. by D. J. Enright and David Rawlinson, Oxford
University Press, 1991; *Naming the Waves: Contemporary Lesbian
Poetry*, ed. by Christian McEwen, London, Virago, 1988; *The Penguin
Book of Homosexual Verse*, ed. by Stephen Coote, London, 1986 edn.

Preparing Services of Blessing and Commitment

The view of an Anglican priest

I have been taking services of blessing for gay and lesbian
couples since 1973. Each time such a service is held my stomach
tightens and I feel apprehensive, not just because the tabloid
press might give unwelcome publicity ('Oddball vicar blesses
gays' – *News of the World*, August 1989) but because I know that
I am flying in the face of two thousand years of Church history
and the majority of my fellow Christians disapprove of what I
am doing. Despite all that, I believe that it is a natural and right
thing to do because God has created a wonderful world full of all
sorts of different people, black, brown, yellow, white, tall, short,
fat, thin, male, female, heterosexual, homosexual. *Vive la différence!*
A large percentage of the human race, somewhere between 5 and
10 per cent, have been made by God with a homosexual
orientation, so it is natural for them to form same-sex relation-

ships. It is also natural that a few of them will come and ask for God's blessings as they form their unions and make their promises to each other.

Over the last twenty years gay men and lesbians have emerged from the shadows and we are beginning to learn about their life-styles. To hear some Christians talk, one would imagine such people are haters instead of lovers. In the two or three preparatory sessions before the service I ask to hear their stories, which always contain much rejection and oppression. The pain some men and women have been subjected to because of their orienta-tion is almost unbearable. Yet they always believe, as I do, that their love is divine in origin and needs to be acknowledged as such in God's house. They want, quite rightly, to thank God for giving them their love and for giving them to each other. Who am I to refuse them? Am I to say their love is wicked, perverse, diseased, sinful in itself? Their life-styles are no better and no worse than those of heterosexual couples. Their love is as deep but different. Nearly always the service has to be held in secret behind locked doors, not because I am ashamed but because I want to protect them from the gutter press who would try to destroy them. Often only the couple are present and sometimes only their very closest friends witness the public affirmation of their relationship. Over the years all sorts of people have come, including the son of a woman whose marriage I took twenty-six years before in Winchester. She had quite a shock when she recognized me! Now nearly always parents will be invited and often they attend and quietly say to me afterwards that they cannot fully understand the relationship but are glad the couple are taking it so seriously and someone in the Church is prepared to pronounce God's blessing on them.

The order of service is tailored to the couple's beliefs and needs. In my experience everyone has asked to make a life-long commitment despite my suggesting they follow the example of monks and nuns and make a one-, three- or five-year commitment. None have opted for 'until we both agree to part'. This obviously means they are taking the service very seriously indeed, as we should. Sometimes symbolism plays a part in the liturgy – tasting salt together (sharing the bitter things of life), drinking wine (the happier days) and eating bread (the ordinary things). Favourite prose, poetry and music is heard, scripture is read and explained, prayers are said and a blessing given. The congregation is asked to affirm the couple's love and promise they will support and help the relationship. There is, of course, no legal part to the service so I usually suggest that, at the exchange of rings, wills are signed in favour of the partners.

I believe it does the lesbian and gay world a disservice to ask them to copy slavishly the model of heterosexual marriage. Some – a minority, I believe – will wish to do this, but most will want the freedom to develop their own unions around their own talents, gifts and shortcomings. The love of each couple is unique and a liturgy of celebration or blessing needs to reflect that.

Since the 1987 debate in the General Synod I have noticed that very few couples ask for a blessing.* Presumably they believe we Christians reject them and would not consider such a service. It seems odd in the decade of evangelism that we have slammed the door in their face.

Malcolm Johnson

The view of a Roman Catholic priest

Doctrinally, the Roman Catholic Church is limited in what it can offer to its homosexual members. But since even in the marriage

---

*In 1987 the Church of England engaged in an extremely public and acrimonious debate on homosexuality, eventually resolving that homosexual genital acts, along with fornication and adultery, fall short of the ideal of marriage and are to be met by a call to repentance and the exercise of compassion.

service there is no explicit mention of the sexual act (although it is implicit in phrases such as '. . . no longer be two, but one flesh' and 'will you accept children lovingly from God?'), it should not be difficult to offer prayers, blessings and other liturgies to meet the legitimate needs of lesbian and gay Catholics.

'Legitimate' is a problematic word. It may be viewed from different viewpoints. For the homosexual impatient to have the Church 'legitimize' a relationship it is a very restrictive word. For the pastor eager to minister to homosexual needs it is a restraining term but none the less binding as the authority of the institution.

Reconciliation of these two points of view can lead to friction. Then it is that the priest has to be at his most sensitive. The basic premise has to be that everything is on offer which is not either forbidden explicitly or at least clearly inappropriate and irreconcilable with accepted Church teaching.

Given today's freedom in the composition of para-liturgies it should not be difficult for the concerned pastor to create or adapt a prayer or blessing to meet the legitimate – again we use that word – aspirations of a lesbian or gay Church member.

The blessing of an automobile is not likely to require adaptation because its owner or driver is homosexual. Nor is the blessing of a house. There may be genuine difficulties when it comes to the blessing of a ring or a union. These would require previous thoughtful discussion to reconcile the elements of the service with the nature of the occasion.

All true liturgy is first and foremost an act of worship within which the needs of the people of God are addressed and sanctified. It is a perversion of liturgy to see it principally as solicitude for the petitioner set in a religious context. The acknowledgement of an almighty God takes precedence.

We live in an overwhelmingly personalized society. We need to recognize community more. For the Christian that community is above all the coming together of the people of God. Their care and concern for one another will reflect the creator's care and concern for them. Individually we may be homosexual or heterosexual. In our community awareness we are neither – at least not initially. We are persons created and blessed by the Father, saved and blessed by the Son, inspired and blessed by the Holy Spirit.

Nowhere should this fundamental relationship be more recognized than within the perception of the ordained pastors of the Church. Their apostolate is to God's people whatever their sexual orientation.

Gay and lesbian Catholics have the freedom and the obligation of any Catholic to participate in the sacramental, liturgical and prayer life of the Church. Where there are needs, it is their right and their pastors' duty to attempt to meet these needs to their fullest possible degree.

Pastors, of course, are not the only resource. Lay ministers are increasingly available within the Church. What has been said of pastors applies equally to all who minister to God's people within the Church.

John Breslin

The view of a Unitarian minister

The phone rings. A woman hesitantly says she has been given my name by Gay Switchboard and will I 'do a marriage'? I ask if she means a heterosexual marriage, or a same-sex union or blessing. She says it's a same-sex union. I explain that this cannot legally be called a marriage, but yes, I am certainly prepared to consider conducting a blessing or affirmation of a same-sex partnership. The law forbids a 'pretend' marriage or a marriage between people of the same sex.

I have found that the answers to a few questions usually

indicate whether or not a service will be appropriate. So I ask how long the couple have known each other and whether either of them is or has been married. If they have been involved in any other serious relationships, I need to satisfy myself that these other commitments are well and truly in the past. I ask their ages. I would not want to perform a union ceremony for men under twenty-one – the age of consent for homosexual sex between men – and although there is no legal age of consent for women, I would not be happy if either of them were very young. We often have a short discussion of what sort of ceremony they have in mind. Before committing myself I arrange to meet both partners, possibly after a Sunday service at the church.

Because Unitarians believe that each person should work out their beliefs in the light of their own experience, we impose no creeds and welcome sincere diversity. So my congregation is open to my conducting services affirming same-sex partnerships. My procedure for working with same-sex and heterosexual partners is basically the same, though for marriages there are some additional formalities – certificates from the registrar, legal wording about 'impediments', promises and registration.

When we meet I explore how seriously committed the couple are to each other. Often they have been living together for some time. I check that both want a service, rather than one partner doing it just to please the other. They generally find it difficult when I ask why they want a service or what they expect a service to do. Answers include confirming commitment and affirming their partnership in front of family and/or friends. If they mention blessing we explore where blessing comes from: does it come from God on high or is it rather something they themselves, with those present, bring to the relationship?

It may seem odd, but I remind couples that as the service is not recognized legally, their seriousness about caring for each other needs to take the practical form of making wills so that each is provided for. The distressing cases known to the Gay Bereavement Project, where the death of a partner has led to loss of home and possessions and exclusion from the funeral, show the need for this.

The central point of the service is the commitment the couple make to each other. So I ask them to think about what is special about their partnership which they want to affirm, and what sort of commitment they wish to make to each other. Are they agreed about how much freedom and space they want? How do they visualize their partnership in five or ten years' time? I generally discourage making promises for life, especially if the partners are young. It is best if they go away and think about all this separately, write it down and bring their thoughts to our next meeting. All these things would also apply to heterosexual couples.

When we meet again we discuss their responses, exploring their differences and similarities, and I help them to put their commitment to each other into words that will be the 'promises' in their service. Each service is unique. A lot depends on whether they want a simple private service, just the three of us, or whether they want to fill the church with friends and family. Most people opt for something in between. The bigger the numbers, the more elaborate the occasion tends to be. It is nice if each partner has a supporter; they may want other attendants and witnesses.

How will we start? Both entering together, both already in or one in first and then the other? There are no rules, only my judgement about what will work, and even then I have been persuaded to risk the unusual – like getting a piper to take up a tune started on the organ; it worked magnificently! What readings shall we choose? Who shall read them – perhaps close friends or family? Parents and children are sometimes delighted to be included in the ceremony. The couple's religious background will affect the sort of language used. Often the general format of the promises and commitment is not very different from those in a conventional marriage, but the specific words are of course different on each occasion. They usually exchange rings. Invariably the couple choose to sign a certificate, often with witnesses, even though in the present state of British law this can have no legal significance.

The sense of celebration, with its blend of deep seriousness and enormous fun and happiness, makes the occasion moving and memorable for all who take part. It is an aspect of my ministry which I particularly value. Not only does it meet people's needs, but more than this it shows the world that alternative life-styles can be valued and worthy of celebration. Unitarians have a traditional loyalty to 'civil and religious liberty', enabling partners of the same sex to celebrate their union is part of my witness to this tradition.

Ann Peart

The view of a Metropolitan Community Church pastor

The Universal Fellowship of Metropolitan Community Churches was founded by the Revd Troy Perry, a former Pentecostal minister, who was asked to leave his church and pulpit when he disclosed the fact that he was gay. It was founded in 1968 in the United States. Troy believed that God was calling him to found a 'house church' in his own living-room, to minister to the needs of his lesbian and gay friends who believed that God did not love them because of their sexuality. MCC now has a membership of more than 27,000 and churches in seventeen different countries. It is estimated that attenders and adherents to MCC churches around the world number around 500,000 people, by no means all of whom are lesbian or gay.

MCC offers two forms of service for couples who are seeking a rite within the Church to bless their relationship. A service of blessing is designed for couples who have been together a short time (under one year) and who desire to make their intentions known, both to one another and before God. A prayer of blessing is said, rings can be exchanged and the couple are encouraged to work together to ensure that their relationship works out.

A service of holy union is offered to couples who have been together, usually for more than one year. Couples who are interested in this kind of service are asked to enter into a time of pre-union counselling. This is designed to help them be sure that this is the kind of long-term commitment that they are ready to make. If the pastor feels that the couple are sufficiently secure and stable, a service of holy union is granted and the couple exchange vows, rings, make promises to one another, sing hymns – in fact a service might resemble a tradi- tional 'wedding', although we encourage couples to find a way which is meaningful to them rather than follow some 'tradi- tion'.

These services, although not recognized by the state, are indeed recognized by God and performed before witnesses who are charged with the responsibility of encouraging their friends, the couple, to continue to work at, and deepen, their commitment to one another. MCC takes these services very seriously and requires that the couple also do so.

MCC is seeking out new ways in which couples, gay and straight, can seek out God's promised love for all people, and as a Church we are developing these resources for the lesbian and gay community. It is important that gay and lesbian people are assured that God is neither heterosexist nor sexist but creates each and every one of us in the divine image. When we can learn and accept this fact, then we shall be able to affirm our love for each other. In relationships, in the Church, MCC is leading the way and others are following on.

Neil Thomas

2

Housewarmings

In his excellent book on the gay and lesbian community, Dr Don Clark has drawn attention to the special significance often attached to gay and lesbian housewarming parties:

For us, marriage comes most often when the two people move into a home together. That housewarming party is a wedding party and every guest who is gay knows it. Gay friends and gay family come with their blessings and hopes for a good future. It is the beginning of a new family unit ... Understanding this helps to explain the mystery about why biological family members are so often reluctant to appear at the housewarming celebration ... To bless the event and wish the future happiness of the couple would be to admit that their community-based prejudice and lack of support has been wrong. (*As We Are*, Boston, Alyson Publications, 1988)

An increasing number of heterosexual couples also opt to live together before or instead of getting married, and for them too a party to celebrate their first home together has enormous significance.

But most couples move home many times in their lives and not only lovers choose to live together — friends, colleagues, relations, students often come together to share a home. Our homes should be places of security, safety, comfort, hospitality and humour. They are places where we should be able to be ourselves; for those who suffer marginalization and rejection in our society because of their sexuality and life-style this is particu-

larly important. Christian people will want to affirm the presence
of God in their new home and commit themselves to realizing
the divine presence in the spirit and activities of the home. The
following suggestions for housewarming liturgies attempt to
express these desires through words and symbols.

1.   *Everyone gathers, if possible, in the hall of the house or flat or in
the main room.*

Early on a Sunday morning women discovered that Jesus was
risen. They were given a message for his disciples . . . 'he is gone
before you to Galilee'. And he goes before us, too, and is here to
greet us, to welcome us as host.

A cross is placed in the middle of the hall or room.

Christ is here. God's spirit is with us.

This is a place of new beginnings, but time past is a part of time
present. In the past lie causes of joy and sorrow. Let us acknowledge the past with thankful hearts.

**This home is a place of welcome, a place of celebration, a
place of meeting, a place of joy and sorrow, a place of rest
and peace.**

Everyone moves to the kitchen.

What else will this home be?

This home is a place of work, the work of hands and head.

What else is this house/flat?

This home is part of the Church, the people of God.

Everyone moves to the dining area.

What else is this home?

This home is a place for sharing – in worship, in caring, in learning, in eating.

Bread and wine are placed on the table.

Gracious God, we offer to you ourselves, our minds and bodies, our home and possessions, our strengths and weaknesses, to share in the life and service of your kingdom. We ask your blessing on everyone and everything that passes through this home.

Amen.

All share a meal.

(Hazel Barkham)

2. *All gather at the door of the home.*

> May the door of this home be wide enough
> to receive all who hunger for love,
> all who are lonely for friendship.
> May it welcome all who have cares to unburden,
> thanks to express, hopes to nurture.
> May the door of this house/flat be narrow enough
> to shut out pettiness and pride, envy and enmity.
> May its threshold be no stumbling block
> to young or strained feet.
> May it be too high to admit complacency,
> selfishness and harshness.
> May this home be for all who enter,
> the doorway to richness and a more meaningful life.

Amen.

(the Siddur of Shir Chadash)

3. *All gather outside the home. The occupants place a pink triangle,*

gay flag or other lesbian or gay symbol on the door of the home and say: Just as the ancient Israelites marked their door lintels with blood as a sign that they were blessed and chosen by God, so we mark our door with a sign of our blessedness as lesbian women/ gay men. The people of Israel marked their doors on the eve of their exodus from slavery into freedom. By marking this house/ flat we identify with them on their journey, for gay and lesbian people are also in the process of coming out of oppression. May everything that happens in this home and all who come into it take us further in our journey towards liberation.

All go into the main room.

God of all creation look down in love on your friends gathered here in N and N's new home. We pray that this home may become the tent of your presence. May it radiate your wholeness, love and peace, your *shalom*. May hate, evil, apathy, narrow-mindedness and destruction find no sanctuary here. Bless and preserve all who live in this house/flat and all who come in and go out of its doors.

Amen.

(Elizabeth Stuart)

This our living space we transform into a home, a place of peace, security and love. Let it be a place of joy, of fruitful work, refreshing relaxation, and strengthening ties with those we love.

(Rosemary Radford Ruether)

Readings

1.   To fear the Lord is the beginning of wisdom;
     she is created with the faithful in the womb.
     She made among human beings an eternal foundation,
     and among their descendants she will abide faithfully.
     To fear the Lord is fullness of wisdom;
     she inebriates mortals with her fruits;
     she fills their whole house with desirable goods,
     and their storehouses with her produce.
     The fear of the Lord is the crown of wisdom,
     making peace and perfect health to flourish.

                                        (Sirach 2.14–18)

2.   And as he sat at dinner in Levi's house, many tax collectors
and sinners were also sitting with Jesus and his disciples – for
there were many who followed him. When the scribes of the
Pharisees saw that he was eating with sinners and tax collectors,
they said to his disciples, 'Why does he eat with tax collectors
and sinners?' When Jesus heard this, he said to them, 'Those who
are well have no need of a physician, but those who are sick; I
have come to call not the righteous but sinners.'

                                        (Mark 2.15–17)

3.   Now as they went on their way, he entered a certain village,
where a woman named Martha welcomed him into her home.
She had a sister named Mary, who sat at the Lord's feet and
listened to what he was saying. But Martha was distracted by her
many tasks; so she came to him and asked, 'Lord, do you not care
that my sister has left me to do all the work by myself? Tell her
to help me.' But the Lord answered her, 'Martha, Martha, you are

worried and distracted by many things; there is need of only one thing. Mary has chosen the better part, which will not be taken away from her.'

(Luke 10.38–42)

4.   Your house is your larger body.
       It grows in the sun and sleeps in the stillness of the
           night; and it is not dreamless. Does not your house
           dream, and dreaming, leave the city for grove
           or hilltop? . . .
       Your house shall be not an anchor but a mast.
       It shall not be a glistening film that covers a wound, but
           an eyelid that guards the eye.
       You shall not fold your wings that you may pass
           through doors, nor bend your heads that they strike
           not against a ceiling, not fear to breathe lest walls
           should crack and fall down.
       You shall not dwell in tombs made by the dead for the
           living.
       And though of magnificence and splendour, your house
           shall not hold your secret nor shelter your longing.
       For that which is boundless in you abides in the mansion
           of the sky, whose door is the morning mist, and
           whose windows are the songs and silences of the
           night.

(Kahlil Gibran)

3

A Celebration of Coming Out

It was the French anthropologist Arnold van Gennep who noted that our lives are made up of a series of passages from one state of being into another and that nearly every one of these events is accompanied by a 'rite of passage', a ceremony to enable the person to pass from one well-defined state of being into another well-defined state of being. The seven sacraments of the Catholic Church can be understood as rites of passage and it is easy to understand the way in which baptism, marriage and funeral services serve this purpose and assure the person in passage of the love and presence of God during this stage of their journey. For a lesbian or gay person the most important passage of their lives is often the process of 'coming out' as a self-affirming lesbian or gay man. Yet, in the Christian tradition, which fails to acknowledge the God-givenness of lesbian and gay sexuality, there has been no rite of passage for them.

Coming out is in fact a life-long process: every day and in many different situations a lesbian or gay person is presented with the choice to deny or acknowledge their sexuality. For every lesbian or gay person who does come out there are thousands who do not. It is easy for those who are 'out' to become terribly self-righteous and judgemental about those who are not. People do not come out for a variety of very good reasons — they may lose jobs, they may be rejected by their family or close friends, they may lose custody of their children.

To some, sexuality is a very personal matter and they feel uncomfortable discussing the subject. Bisexual people may not want to identify with only one end of the spectrum of sexualities. For some people it can be traumatic enough just to come out to oneself. Those of us who have come out need those who have not to remind us of who and what lesbian and gay liberation is for. We must offer friendship and support and not burden them with more guilt. Coming out is only a good and positive action if it is done voluntarily.

The first time a person comes out is a particularly significant occasion. It usually occurs as the result of and the climax to a long and uncomfortable struggle with and against a society (supported by mainstream Christian churches) which seeks to deny the goodness of lesbian and gay sexuality and labels those endowed with it as 'perverted', 'sick', 'sinful' and 'dangerous'. Gay men and lesbian women cannot but help internalize this negativity to at least some degree, and so the battle against self-hatred is also part of the struggle. To come out, therefore, is to make a statement with profound theological, psychological and political implications.

To come out is to say that the Church has got it wrong, that homosexuality is a God-given gift to be rejoiced in, not denied. To come out is to say that society (perhaps including one's own family and closest friends) has got it wrong; that being gay is OK. To come out is to make a huge political, even revolutionary statement, for it is to challenge those who claim authority over us and it is to defy their understanding of reality. It is therefore a risky act and many have paid the price by losing jobs, friends, children and even lives. Unless people do take the risk to break the walls of silence and invisibility that surround homosexuality and echo Luther in declaring 'Here stand I: I can do no other', society and Church will not change. Coming out is too significant an act not to have a rite of passage associated with it.

Coming out implies leaving something behind, 'the closet' of self-hatred, the conspiracy of silence and invisibility, the tomb of self-denial. An important part of coming out is the recognition of the ways in the past in which we have contributed to and colluded with our own marginalization and that of our countless gay and lesbian brothers and sisters. This is why I have included rites of reflection and repentance in the material in this section.

All rites of passage are communal events because we need the support and love of others to help us through the process of moving from the old into the new. When a lesbian or gay man comes out voluntarily, they usually do so partly as a result of good experiences of support from other lesbians or gay men. It is important therefore that these friends are present. They are also coming into the lesbian and gay community which is their community and which needs them to join in the struggle for liberation. The community should therefore have a presence in a 'coming-out' rite to welcome the new member.

The symbolism I have used at the centre of this rite is Easter symbolism; darkness and silence give way to light, flowers, colour and music. I think this symbolism appropriate because, as I say in one of the readings suggested for this rite, many people experience coming out as a new birth, a resurrection when deathly denial and self-hatred are thrown off in favour of life-giving self-affirmation and celebration and freedom to be. Who would dare say that God was not present in the experience of resurrection?

Introductions

1.   Dear friends, all life is sacred and a blessed gift. We are here today to give thanks for the gift of life and to bless the life of N,

who has invited us to join her/him in celebrating her/his affirmation of her/himself as a lesbian woman/gay man. In this time when lesbians and gay men are rejected and oppressed our gathering here is a protest against unjust persecution and false judgement. We renounce the homophobia of the Church and proclaim the sacred worth of every child of the Holy One.

(Rebecca Parker and Joanne Brown)

2. 'And alien tears will fill for him pity's long broken urn, for his mourners will be outcast men and outcasts always mourn.' These words are written on the tomb of Oscar Wilde, one of the most famous 'out' gay people of all time. He is buried in France in permanent exile, unwelcome in his own country. We are here today to show that it doesn't have to be like that, that despite living in a society and being part of a Church in which we are often unwelcome and feared we are not doomed to a life of mourning. We come here to give witness to the fact that our sexuality is a gift from God and that we rejoice in the opportunities it gives us to love and relate and enjoy friendships unshackled from the bonds of conformity and socialization. We today declare our pride in belonging to a community of lovers who co-operate with God in building up the divine commonwealth of peace, freedom, love, justice, and equality. We come here today refusing to be victims, refusing to be disempowered and marginalized into a life of mourning. And we come to welcome N into the lesbian and gay community. We pay tribute to his/her courage in coming out and we pledge to support him/her through all the joys and pains of being lesbian or gay in our world today. We pray for God's blessing upon him/her and upon us.

(Elizabeth Stuart)

3. Welcome to this joyous occasion. We come together to celebrate N's decision to publicly name her/himself as lesbian/

gay. Coming out is a process of movement from a denial of who we are to a recognition and celebration of our essential being. It is a process that never ends. Every day of our lives we are faced with the decision of whether to deny our sexuality or declare it. But the first time we come out is a particularly sacred moment in which we experience a foretaste of the resurrection. We emerge from a state of fear, denial, pain, isolation and confusion into a new life of affirmation, love, joy and community. We give thanks to God for leading N out of exile into freedom and out of death into life.

(Elizabeth Stuart)

Rite of Repentance

'I do not know or understand what you are talking about.' These are the words of Peter the first time he denied Jesus. We remember those times when we have denied God and the divine gift of our sexuality by pretending to know or understanding nothing about homosexuality.

Kyrie eleison, Christe eleison. (Lord have mercy, Christ have mercy.)

'And the servant-girl, on seeing him, began again to say to the bystanders, "This man is one of them." But again he denied it.' Peter's second denial. We remember those times when we have denied that we were 'one of them'. The times when we have smiled at and even joined in the anti-gay jokes for fear of being exposed as one of them. The times when we have betrayed God our creator, ourselves and our gay brothers and lesbian sisters by denying implicitly or explicitly that we are 'one of them'.

Kyrie eleison, Christe eleison.

'But he began to curse, and he swore an oath. "I do not know this person you are talking about."' We remember those times when confronted by our inner selves, our family or friends we have lied and unambiguously denied our sexuality. Like Peter, there are many times when we have broken down and wept, crucified by our own fear of who we are.

Kyrie eleison, Christe eleison.

Like Peter, we repent of the times when we have denied God, ourselves and each other. And like Peter we receive God's forgiveness and command to work for the furtherance of his commonwealth by celebrating who we are and working for a world in which all will enjoy the freedom to be.

(Elizabeth Stuart)

The Declaration of Coming Out

The room should be darkened.

The person coming out: As Eve came out of Adam, as the people of Israel came out of slavery into freedom, as the exiled Israelites came out of Babylon back to their home, as Lazarus came out of the tomb to continue his life, as Jesus came out of death into new life I come out – out of the desert into the garden, out of the darkness into light, out of exile into my home, out of lies into the truth, out of denial into affirmation. I name myself as gay/lesbian. Blessed be God who has made me so.

The person coming out lights a candle and all present light their candles from it. Colourful flowers are brought in. Music is played or a song sung. The whole room should be filled with light, colour and music.

(Elizabeth Stuart)

Psalms

1.   O, Lord you have searched me and known me.
      You know when I sit down and when I rise up
      you discern my thoughts from far away.
      You search out my path and my lying down,
      and are acquainted with all my ways.
      Even before a word is on my tongue,
      O Lord, you know it completely.
      You hem me in, behind and before
      and lay your hand upon me.
      Such knowledge is too wonderful for me;
      it is so high that I cannot attain it.

      Where can I go from your spirit?
      Or where can I flee from your presence?
      If I ascend to heaven, you are there;
      if I make my bed in Sheol, you are there.
      If I take the wings of the morning
      and settle at the farthest limits of the sea,
      even there your hand shall lead me,
      and your right hand shall hold me fast.
      If I say, 'Surely the darkness shall cover me,
      and the light around me become night,'
      even the darkness is not dark to you;
      the night is as bright as the day,
      for darkness is as light to you.

For it was you who formed my inward parts;
you knit me together in my mother's womb.
I praise you, for I am fearfully and wonderfully made.

(Psalm 139.1–14)

2. Bless the Lord, O my soul,
    and all that is within me,
    bless his holy name.
    Bless the Lord, O my soul,
    and do not forget all his benefits –
    who forgives all your iniquity,
    who heals all diseases,
    who claims your life from the Pit,
    who crowns you with steadfast love and mercy,
    who satisfies you with good as long as you live,
    so that your youth is renewed as an eagle's.
    The Lord works vindication and justice for all who are op-
        pressed.
    He made known his ways to Moses, his acts to the
        people of Israel.
    The Lord is merciful and gracious, slow to anger and
        abounding in steadfast love.

(Psalm 103.1–8)

The Ritual of Welcome

In the name of God the creator who has made you in the divine
image and delights in the diversity of creation, in the name of
God the liberator who breaks the bonds of oppression, in the
name of God the love-maker who rejoices in true love wherever
it is found, we welcome you into the lesbian and gay community
and promise to do all we can to support and sustain you in the

days to come. With you we commit ourselves to integrity and promise to fight ignorance, injustice and fear wherever it is found.

We now share together bread and wine. These are the symbols of God's commonwealth where all shall live together free from pain, exploitation and oppression, delighting in the diversity of God's creation. By sharing the bread and wine today we recognize that what we are celebrating today takes humankind one more step along the road towards that goal.

Bread and wine are shared.

(Elizabeth Stuart)

Prayers

1.   A priest sent a card of van Gogh's 'Olive Orchard'.
       In the tortured brush strokes,
       the artist reveals his own agony
       as he depicts Christ's agony in Gethsemane.
       The priest sees in the reproduction
       his own spiritual struggle to accept his homosexuality.

       Let us pray for this priest
       and the many like him
       who are part of an invisible community of suffering,
       unknown, unfelt, unloved by the Church:

       We pray, O God, for those who live in closets.

       For the two hundred and twenty thousand homosexuals
       murdered in Nazi concentration camps

and those who remained imprisoned despite the allied vic-
tory,
who now live in history's closet:

We pray, O God, for those who died in closets.

For millions of lesbians and gay men in other countries
in which there are no support systems or groups,
in which revelation leads to imprisonment, castration, or
death:

We pray, O God, for those who fear in closets.

For priests, nuns, ministers, and lay Church leaders
who, to serve the Church, cannot come out,
while bringing liberation to others who are oppressed:

**We pray, O God, for those who liberate from
closets.**

For spouses, who also must hide — non-gay spouses,
protective of their loved ones' careers, gay lovers,
hiding their love under a bushel:

We pray, O God, for those who love in closets.

Thank you, God, for all who, throughout the world,
struggle to make Churches and cultures more inclusive,
homes where there are no strangers.

**O God, may closets go the way of the Berlin Wall.
Alleluia! Amen.**

(Chris Glaser)

2.   O God of truth and justice, the evasions and deceits we
practise upon others and upon ourselves are many.
   We long only to speak and to hear the truth, yet time and

again, from fear of loss or hope of gain, from dull habit or from cruel deliberation, we speak half-truths, we twist facts, we stay silent when others lie, and we lie to ourselves.

Those of us who are lesbian or gay often feel forced to pretend to be that which we are not, to present ourselves in ways which are not truthful, and sometimes with outright lies.

But as we stand before you, our words and our thought speed to One who knows them before we utter them. We do not have to tell untruths to you as we are often forced to do in the straight world. We know we cannot lie in your presence.

May our worship help us to practise truth in speech and thought before you, to ourselves, and before one another; and may we finally complete our liberation so that we no longer feel the need to practise evasions and deceits.

(Rebecca Parker and Joanne Brown)

3.   God we believe; we have told you we believe ... We have not denied you, then rise up and defend us. Acknowledge us, oh God, before the whole world. Give us also the right to our existence!

(Radclyffe Hall)

Final Blessing

All join hands.

May the God of the exodus who continually leads us from slavery to freedom, from darkness to light, from death to life, bless us and keep us faithful to the cause of the commonwealth.

(Elizabeth Stuart)

Readings

1. You are the light of the world. A city built on a hill cannot be hid. No one after lighting a lamp puts it under the bushel basket, but on the lampstand, and it gives light to all in the house. In the same way, let your light shine before others, so that they may see your good works and give glory to your Father in heaven.

(Matthew 5.14–16)

2. I've heard a number of people comparing their experience of coming out with being born again. I would like to consider the story of Easter, the story of resurrection of the body first experienced by Christ, from the perspective of coming out.

Then Joseph bought a linen cloth, and taking down the body, wrapped it in the linen cloth, and laid it in a tomb that had been hewn out of the rock. He then rolled a stone against the door of the tomb. (Mark 15.46)

Many of us spend a period of our lives feeling entombed in our bodies. We are afraid and ashamed of our sexuality and would do anything to escape from the condemnation and hurt that it causes us. We feel totally and utterly alone, utterly isolated from a world and a Church that cannot accept us as we are. And we are bound with the grave clothes of socialization. We have been brought up to believe that it is unacceptable to be gay or lesbian, that it is impossible for people like us to be happy, to settle down with a partner, to have families, to avoid AIDS and so on. We are taught to hate ourselves. Bound up by these beliefs we live a lie, a half-life; in fact we don't really live at all because we are attempting to kill, maim or silence the essential part of ourselves, the part of ourselves that allows us to relate to other people, to God and to our own beings. We are locked into a cold, dark prison of death. Some of us stay in the tomb for the whole of our lives.

When they looked up, they saw that the stone, which was very large, had already been rolled back. As they entered the tomb, they saw a young man, dressed in a white robe, sitting on the right side; and they were alarmed. But he said to them, 'Do not be alarmed; you are looking for Jesus of Nazareth, who was crucified. He has been raised; he is not here . . .' (Mark 16.4–6)

It may happen slowly or it may come quite suddenly and unexpectedly, the realization that you are entombed but you need not be, the realization that you are accepted and loved as you are, the realization that what you thought was evil, corrupting, life-denying is in fact good, liberating and life-giving. We unwind the grave clothes of socialization and of Church teaching recognizing them for what they are, bonds to keep us dead, to keep us lying down, to keep us out of the way and powerless. And our 'angels', our friends and lovers, help us to roll away the stone of fear and we burst out of the tomb of self-hatred into new life. We emerge as liberated people lit up with the light of self-love. Only our friends can recognize us as resurrected and liberated. Our foes continually try to push us back into the darkness, into the tomb, not understanding that the darkness can no longer overcome the light. We travel through the world lighting it up with our love but still bearing the scars of our crucifixion and entombment in order to call the world to repentance for failing to recognize the image of God in us and also to be signs of hope to those still locked away.

(Elizabeth Stuart)

3. Coming out, I come into the realization of myself as best able to relate most intimately – to touch and be touched most deeply, to give and receive most naturally, to empower

and be empowered most remarkably, to express everything I most value: God in human life, God in justice, God in passion, God as love — in sexual relationship to a lover who is female. . . .

Coming out, there are things lost: the likelihood of bearing my own children and learning how to live better with male lovers. But the gain outweighs the loss: Coming out, I begin to envision and embrace the children of the world as my own and the men of the world as my brothers, whom I can better learn to know and love as friends. Coming out involves a recognition of the creative power I have always experienced in relation to women. Coming out is a confession that I need and want intimacy with someone whose values and ways of being in the world can support and be supported by my own. Coming out means realizing and cherishing my parents' way of loving and of being in the world, of valuing who they have been and who they are, and of knowing myself both as bound to them and as separate from them in journeying. Coming out means remembering my other relatives and early friends in the hope that they can trust and celebrate the parts we have played in the shaping of one another's values.

Coming out is a protest against social structures that are built on alienation between men and women, women and women, men and men. Coming out is the most radical, deeply personal and consciously political affirmation I can make on behalf of the possibilities of love and justice in the social order. Coming out is moving into relation with peers. It is not simply a way of being in bed, but rather a way of being in the world. To the extent that it invites voyeurism, coming out is an invitation to look and see and consider the value of mutuality in human life. Coming out is simultaneously a political movement and the mighty rush of God's Spirit carrying us on.

Coming out, I stake my sexual identity on the claim that I

hold to be the gospel at its heart: that we are here to love God
and our neighbours as ourselves. Each of us must find her or his
own way to the realization of this claim.

(Carter Heyward)

4.   The sacrament of 'coming out' is a kind of letting go: a
letting go of the images of personhood, sexuality and selfhood
that society has put on one in favour of trusting oneself enough
to let oneself be oneself. Just as the slave had to empty himself
or herself of the slave master's language and thinking and value
system, so too the homosexual undergoes emptying of a profound personal and social kind of projects and projections that
heterosexual society has insisted on. This emptying and letting
go and letting be can lead either to a deeper and more vulnerable,
more compassionate sense of belonging with others who suffer
unjustly − or it can lead to a cynicism, a rage, a hoarding of
consumer idols including sexual consumerism on the part of the
homosexual. If it leads to the former it is certainly a blessing in
disguise, a school of wisdom learned by suffering, a theology of
the apophatic God, the God of darkness, whom the straight
world needs so desperately to hear more about.

(Matthew Fox)

5.   My voice rings down through thousands of years
     To coil around your body and give you strength,
     You who have wept in direct sunlight,
     Who have hungered in invisible chains,
     Tremble to the cadence of my legacy:
     An army of lovers shall not fail.

(Rita Mae Brown)

4

Partings

Many people need help today in the rituals of endings and new beginnings. As someone who has been divorced, I know that we need rituals to free us from domination by our past failures and to reincorporate us in the new humanity of Christ.[1]

Relationships end. Marriages break up, partnerships both hetero-sexual and homosexual die, friendships are severed. By no means all relationships end; some indeed are lifelong, and of these some are by and large happy and some are not. The bald fact is that many of us experience the pain and despair of parting from the person who had been our 'significant other' at least once in our lives. Many of these relationships will have been celebrated and formalized in a liturgical setting or in some other solemn manner. Relationships break down for a whole variety of reasons, but the process is always traumatic for those involved, however 'civilized' the relationship between the former partners. For those going through a divorce one of the most difficult things to cope with, as Robin Green makes clear, is that there is no fixed point, apart from appearance in court, at which the marriage can be declared to be at an end before the world. For heterosexual couples who have not married, for gay or lesbian couples and for close friends who have not had a sexual relationship, there is not even the formality of the legal process to help them formally break the bonds between them. For all these people there is no point at which the couple can stand together in front of the family and friends who celebrated and supported their relationship and say to each other: 'This is the end, we both have to start again, but I want to acknowledge and give thanks for the love you gave me and the good times we had and I want to ask forgiveness for the pain and hurt I have caused you.' There is a great need to face up formally to failure and tied up loose ends, in order to be able to start again. Many will also need to experience the healing and strengthening love of God at such a time. They will need to know that God is not a divorce-court judge who apportions blame but an unconditional lover who desires wholeness, not brokenness, love, not hate, and would not take any delight in a destructive, diminishing, imprisoning relationship.

The Church has failed to provide liturgical opportunities for those going through a parting to make sense of their experience. Divorce has been discouraged on the basis of Jesus' apparent condemnation of it (Mark 10.2–10) and relationships outside of marriage have not been recognized. It is telling that thousands of Christian men and women have been shunned, deprived of the sacraments and made to feel unwelcome in the Church because they are divorced. It has often seemed that divorced people were deprived of the forgiveness offered to others whose behaviour Jesus also condemned. Jesus was anything but a legalist, and I have no doubt that he would have understood, welcomed, loved and defended those fleeing from a destructive relationship. Unfortunately his Church has not always understood this and many men and women have paid the price.

In this section I have brought together liturgical material which could be used by heterosexual and gay or lesbian couples, companions and friends to formalize the ending of their significant relationship. In such a traumatic and painful situation words are often simply not enough to express the depth and variety of feelings felt by all parties, which is why I would suggest that a parting liturgy should centre around a symbolic dramatization of the ending of the relationship which expresses the hurt, pain, sense of failure and tragedy of the occasion, and also the beginning of something new. Without death we cannot rise into new life. We need to bury the relationship and that means acknowledging the pain and hurt and failure but also celebrating the good and granting forgiveness. I hope that the material presented here will enable some to experience God's presence and love in the mess of parting and be able to respond to God's challenge to 'follow me' into an unknown future and new beginning.

Introduction

1. Welcome to all who have been drawn here out of love for N and N. We, their family and friends, join them today to mark the end of their commitment, and to ask God's blessing upon them as they face the challenge of a new journey. May the Holy One grace them now and with loving kindness in the days to come.

(Florence Perrella Hayes)

Rituals and Pronouncement of Separation

1. *Each partner in turn*: N, I do hereby affirm my place in this ending of our commitment. From this day our ways separate and our loves part. Now I enter into a new relationship with you. I shall treasure always the things we shared that were beautiful. At the same time, I shall hold as valuable and worthy the new and happy things in your life ahead. Above all, I promise to respect you as an individual. We have hurt each other and been hurt.

Knowing your strengths and weaknesses, I shall see and honour and treat you as a person. This is my pledge.

(adapted from Rudolph W. Nemser)

The rings or gifts that were exchanged at the celebration of their commitment are given to the leader.

2.   *The couple take a seed as the symbol of their love which they planted together and nutured while it grew and matured into life. Now it must die in order to bring new life. They both place it in a bowl of earth and bury it together.*

3.   *The couple each take a mug, a plate or another piece of china which belongs to them both. Each in turn say*: N, I entered willingly into our relationship as lovers. I now mark the end of that relationship of my own free will. This is the symbol of our sharing of happy times and sad times. I smash it to show the end of our life together, the fracturing of our dreams of a shared future. With its breaking may your hurt and my hurt be seen and may bitterness and anger also come to an end.

The china is smashed on the floor or with a hammer and a friend or minister says: Let this symbolic act be the freeing from a pledge once undertaken and now outlived. God blessed your commitment to each other, but God has no wish to lock you in a relationship that no longer nurtures, sustains or delights you. God calls us to creativity, growth, wholeness and joy. For you, that call now leads you out of this relationship into the unknown. Be assured of God's continued presence and love. For God has said:

> You are my servant, I have chosen you and not cast you off; do not fear, for I am with you, do not be afraid, for I am your

God; I will strengthen you, I will help you, I will uphold you with my victorious right hand. (Isaiah 41.9–10)

You are now free to enter a new life, a new commitment, a new love again. Go forth, not in the hurt of ties wrenched and faith unachieved, but with hope and belief in love yet possible and ties still to be found and held.

(Elizabeth Stuart)

Prayers

1. Eternal friend, for whom a thousand years are but a day, watch with me now as I begin all over again. The months (and years) with N – all that hope and happiness – have fallen from my life like wasted time. And I feel older not wiser. Give me comfort and the courage to go forward without denying the past, to learn from what I have lost without being crushed by it.

(Jane Robson)

2. After so many words – the confusion, sorrow, anger, hatred or reproach – may all tongues now fall silent as we contemplate what was God-given and Christ-like in our beginning and in our living together. May God's Holy Spirit be with each of us and bless us as we travel our new and separate paths.

(Jane Robson)

3. Lord take away this cup of bitterness. Break my anger as my heart has been broken. In the darkness of my hurt let there be hope. And one day, perhaps, let there be love again.

(Jane Robson)

4.   For giving up on love, for the resenting and the betrayals and the loss of trust,

Lord, have mercy.

For not speaking soon enough when small things were wrong and for attacking so quickly and cruelly when it was too late,

Christ, have mercy.

On the memory of our time together, and the wrong we have done each other, and our vulnerability.

Friend, have mercy.

(Jane Robson)

The Pronouncement of Separation

And so, as you, N and N, have stated to one another your intention to live apart and to create lives independent of one another; as you have further declared your common commitment to the health and well-being of one another and to the good of all your lives will touch; and as you, finally, have declared your pledge of trustworthiness – to respect yourselves and each other: I now pronounce your commitment dissolved.

I summon you in the name of God the maker of love, God the pain-bearer, God the bringer of forgiveness and resurrection, in the days that lie ahead, dark days and bright days, to recall the vision and hopes of this moment.

I summon your families and friends to treat now and forever as sacred the decision you have made and the courses ahead which you have chosen. I summon them to mediate God's love and concern to you both. Do you promise to do so?

We do.

(Rudolph W. Nemser)

Final Prayer and Blessing

O God our comfort and challenge,
whose presence is ever reliable
and ever unexpected;
grant us to grieve over what is ending
without falling into despair,
and to enter on our new vocation
without forgetting your voice,
through Jesus Christ.

Amen.

(Janet Morley)

May the God who brings light out of darkness, order out of
chaos, wholeness out of brokenness, life out of death, bless us
with her transforming love now and through all life's endings.

Amen.

(Elizabeth Stuart)

Readings

1. Save me, O God, for the waters have come up to my
    neck.
    I sink in deep mire, where there is no foothold;
    I have come into deep waters, and the flood sweeps
    over me.
    I am weary with my crying; my throat is parched.
    My eyes grow dim with waiting for my God . . .

But as for me, my prayer is to you, O Lord.

At an acceptable time, O God, in the abundance of your
   steadfast love, answer me.

With your faithful help rescue me from sinking in the
   mire;

let me be delivered from my enemies and from the deep
   waters.

Do not let the flood sweep over me, or the deep
   swallow me up,

or the Pit close its mouth over me.

(Psalm 69.1–3, 13–15)

2.   Out of the depths I cry to you, O Lord.

Lord, hear my voice!

Let your ears be attentive to the voice of my supplica-
   tions!

If you, O Lord, should mark iniquities, Lord, who should
   stand?

But there is forgiveness with you, so that you may be
   revered.

I wait for the Lord, my soul waits, and in his word I
   hope;

my soul waits for the Lord more than those who watch
   for the morning,

more than those who watch for the morning.

O Israel, hope in the Lord!

For with the Lord there is steadfast love, and with him is
   great power to redeem.

It is he who will redeem Israel from all its iniquities.

(Psalm 130)

3.   Be gentle with your wounds.
Remember that wounds always leave their mark –
even the emotional hurts are still trapped
in the cells and muscles of your organism.
You can slide over them of course,
even be physically sexual,
and yet remain on the rigid surface,
not allowing the wounds to be touched,
and so getting by with short-lived excitement.
But you need to let the wounds be touched
by a healing love,
and you won't be able to do this
until you trust the healing lover enough
to be assured that your opening up
will not be to further the pain.

                                                     (Jim Cotter)

4.   If I could conjure you precisely
would that relieve me of the loss?
Repeatedly I say to myself,
But I thought this was going to happen,
we were going to do that.

I must now believe in the death
of my old delighted hopes and certainties
and forget the promises
and remember we both tried
and forgive your confusion
and not hate her who took what was most precious
from me.

Oh, lesbian divorce! You death,
you fooler! It was women I believed in

as if we would hurt each other less
than men hurt us.

Sky of my room,
air between the walls,
with what will I fill you now
that I can love no one,
can kiss no one honestly?
I am wide as the unknown distances above
and my space is black and frightening.
I could yell or paint or turn music up
or dance or lie down on the rug
or invite the ones who want me home.

But my lover was a child
and I am a child
and my years are collecting behind me
like the mysteries I love and fear
that are beyond the sunset,
and I'm not ready to rise up born again
like a child learning to walk,
and I'm not ready to have lost her,
and I can't say to the world, *Help me, I am divorced,*
I am divorced!

They would not even believe
we had ever been married.

(Rebecca Lewin)

5. After a while you learn
    The subtle difference
    Between holding a hand
    And chaining a soul.
    And you learn

That love doesn't mean leaning
And company doesn't mean security.
And you begin to learn
That kisses aren't compromises
And presents aren't promises.
And you begin to accept your defeats
With your head up and your eyes ahead
With the grace of a woman or man
Not the grief of a child.
And you learn to build all your loads on today
Because tomorrow's ground is too uncertain for plans
And futures have a way of falling down in midflight.
After a while you learn
That even sunshine burns if you ask too much.
So you plant your own garden
And decorate your own soul
Instead of waiting for someone to bring you flowers.
And you learn
That you really can endure
That you really are strong
And you really do have worth.
And you learn.
And you learn.
With every failure you learn.

                                        (anonymous)

6.   Forgiveness is understanding and holding the pain of an-
         other;
      it is compassion.
     Forgiveness is the acceptance of our brokenness, yours
         and mine.
     Forgiveness is letting go of unrealistic expectations of
         others

and of the desire that they be other than they are.
Forgiveness is liberating others to be themselves, not
   making them feel
guilty for what may have been . . .
Forgiveness is peace-making:
struggling to create unity,
to build one body,
to heal the broken body of humanity.

(Jean Vanier)

The following poems are also offered as suggested readings:

e.e. cummings, 'it may not always be so' and 'i say'; Ernest Dowson, 'A Valediction' and 'Exile'; Henry King, 'The Surrender'; Philip Larkin, 'Talking in Bed'; Kate Hall, 'Psychic Healing', 'Kim', 'Lesbian Strength', and other poems from *Naming the Waves: Contemporary Lesbian Poetry*, ed. by Christian McEwen, London, Virago, 1988; *The Penguin Book of Homosexual Verse*, ed. by Stephen Coote, Harmondsworth, 1986; *The Oxford Book of Friendship*, ed. by D. J. Enright and David Rawlinson, Oxford University Press, 1991.

5

Healing Liturgies for People Living with HIV and AIDS

For the last decade the awful spectre of AIDS has haunted the world. Every person who has had one or more sexual partners during the last ten years, or shared needles in the taking of drugs or has had an untreated blood transfusion has been potentially exposed to the HIV virus. Men, women, children, gay, lesbian, bisexual and heterosexual people, young and old, rich and poor, black or white, the whole community is affected by AIDS. It is important to emphasize this fact because there is still a tendency in the West to perceive HIV disease as the 'gay plague', despite all the evidence to the contrary. But because originally in the West it was gay men who were most affected by the disease and because AIDS brings together the two great taboo subjects in our culture, sexuality and death, people living with the virus and those close to them have often had to suffer the most appalling discrimination and treatment from institutions, friends and even family. The claim by some Christians that AIDS was sent by God, as a punishment for sinful sexual behaviour, did not help. Fortunately the major Christian denominations disowned this approach and argued for non-judgemental support and care for those affected by HIV.

Because of the peculiar nature and history of the AIDS pandemic and the experience of those affected by it, the traditional healing services of the main Christian denominations seemed inadequate and so interested parties began to develop liturgical resources to reflect the experience of those living with HIV — some of these are collected in this section of the book. The World Health Organization has designated the first of December as World AIDS Day in an attempt to raise public awareness of the condition. More and more churches are com-memorating the day with services or vigils for those living with HIV. Some churches now hold regular healing services for people who are HIV + or have AIDS, and these people also hold their own services. I hope that the material in this section will be useful in these contexts. I also hope that some of the prayers in this section will be used in the course of usual Sunday services, for whilst one person has AIDS the whole body of Christ has AIDS and we have a responsibility to care, support and pray for each other.

Some may question the wisdom of seeking healing for a disease for which, at present, there is no cure. However, healing does not necessarily involve a cure, as Jurgen Moltmann has noted in *The Power of the Powerless* (London, SCM, 1983):

True health is the strength to live, the strength to suffer and the strength to die. Health is not a condition of my body, it is the power of my soul to cope with the varying conditions of that body.

It is for this health that we pray for those with the virus, their loved ones and those who care for them.

Mention is made below of a memorial quilt: this is made up of sections of material upon which is embroidered or painted the name of a person who has died of AIDS and perhaps a picture of them or symbols of their lives. As well as being unfurled at the time of remembrance, these quilts can also be used as altar cloths.

The shining of light in the darkness is a powerful symbol of hope in the power of life over death and can also be used as a form of remembrance. So I have included a candle-lighting ceremony in the material.

The anointing with oil is rich in symbolism. In the ancient Jewish world guests were anointed with oil as a sign of welcome. Oil was also the symbol of priesthood and kingship in the Old Testament, a sign of selection to fulfil God's purpose. It could be a symbol of death in the ancient world: corpses were anointed with oil. And finally, oil was also a symbol of healing and wholeness. So anointing a person with oil conveys a rich message: that God welcomes, loves and values them and that they have their part to play in doing God's work; that death must be faced up to and that God offers true health and the strength to live and die as well as possible. Anointing need not be confined to the person carrying the virus. Those caring for them also need strength, support and assurance of God's love.

In 1986 Cardinal Joseph Bernardin of Chicago issued a *Pastoral Statement on AIDS*, in which he wrote:

I know that the fear and pain can be great, but we are a community whose Master's love was so pervasive that it broke through all barriers – those created by society as well as those built up in the human heart. Our responsibility and challenge is to overcome ignorance and prejudice, to become a community of healing and reconciliation in which those who are suffering from AIDS can move from a sense of alienation to one of unity, from a sense of judgement to one of unconditional love.

It is in order to help the Church become a community of reconciliation and healing for those affected by HIV, whatever their sexuality, that this section is included.

Calls to Worship

1. We gather as a people who have experienced the reality of AIDS in our lives.

We know well the confusion and frustration, the loss and the anger, the stigma and discrimination which are part of the reality of AIDS in our lives.

We gather in this place seeking to have our spirits strengthened and our hopes renewed.

Be present with us, life-giving Spirit, and be for us the source of strength, courage, and hope. Come, Holy Spirit! Revive us again!

(Louis F. Kavar)

2.   God is with us! Listen, all people, and be humble; for God is with us!

Give ear, all you lands afar off; God is with us!

God is with us! Listen, all people, and be humble; for God is with us!

You rulers of the world, be humble; even if your arrogance returns, you will be humbled again; for God is with us!

God is with us! Listen, all people, and be humble; for God is with us!

O rulers and those in power, whatever conspiracy you weave, Yahweh shall destroy it; whatever word you speak shall not stand even among you; for God is with us!

God is with us! Listen, all people, and be humble; for God is with us!

We shall not hear your threat, nor shall we be disturbed; we glorify the name of Yahweh, our God; for God is with us!

God is with us! Listen, all people, and be humble; for God is with us!

O people who are walking in gloom, expect to see a great light;
for God is with us!

**God is with us! Listen, all people, and be humble; for God is
with us!**

Upon us who dwell in the land of the shadow of death a great
light shall dawn; for God is with us!

**God is with us! Give ear, all you nations, and be humbled;
for God is with us!**

(Louis F. Kavar)

The Lighting of Candles

*The leader lights a candle and lights the candles of two people in the
congregation who then light the candles of those beside them and so the
process goes on until all have lighted candles. As this is done the
following is said:* We live in many darknesses. We are often
uncertain. We are sometimes afraid.

In the darkness, we light a candle of hope.

We all have sorrows. We have known pain. Each of us carries
special regrets.

In our pain, we light a candle of forgiveness.

We are sometimes lonely, and the world seems cold and hard.

In our loneliness, we light a candle of thanks.

We have known awe, wonder, mystery; glimmerings of perfection
in our imperfect world.

In our wonder, we light a candle of praise.

We bring together many uncertainties, many sorrows, many joys, much wonder.

We bring together many candles, many lights.

May our separate lights become one flame, that together we may be nourished by its glow.

(from an interfaith celebration of love)

Prayers

1.   God calls us as a people in whom no one is expendable. We are called to bear witness to the good news that no one is a stranger or outsider; that in Jesus all division and separation have been broken down. In the face of the world crisis of AIDS, we are called to be one people and yet hardness of heart, discrimination and oppression prevent us from being whom God calls us to be. For this we seek forgiveness.

God of compassion, we often misrepresent you as a God of wrath, yet you are the God of love, raising us all to life; and so we ask:

Jesus, remember me when you come into your kingdom.

Lord Jesus, you banish the fear that has paralysed us, your Church, in responding to the needs of all who are affected by HIV or AIDS. When we falter, encourage us and strengthen us; and so we ask:

Jesus, remember me when you come into your kingdom.

Spirit of unity, you build us up when we break down; you gather in when we exclude; you affirm when we condemn; and so we ask:

Jesus, remember me when you come into your kingdom.

(Catholic AIDS Link)

2. As those who keep the night watch look for dawn,
    so, Lord, we look for your help.
    May a cure be found;
    May we live positively;
    May we find love to strengthen us
    and free us from fear;
    In the name of him who by dying
    and rising again conquered death
    and is with us now, Jesus Christ.

    Amen.

    (Ecumenical AIDS Support Team, Edinburgh)

3. Great God who has given us life, we have long been taught of your faithfulness and care. We know that you long to gather us as a mother hen gathers her brood. When we have been lost in our confusion, we have found you to be the good shepherd who seeks us until we are found. We remember the times when you securely carried us on your shoulders, rescuing us from the perils of self-doubt and self-hate. Yet, confronted by AIDS, we have often failed to remember that your presence is with us. We have allowed the pain we have experienced to keep us from sharing in the goodness you continue to offer us each day. Forgive us for our lack of constancy, for failing to fix our vision on the promise that indeed nothing can separate us from your love, not even AIDS.

    (Louis F. Kavar)

4. Almighty God, creator of life, sustainer of every good thing we know, our partner with us in the pain of this earth, hear our prayer as we are in the midst of separation and alienation from everything we know to be supportive, and healing, and true.

AIDS has caused me to feel separated from you. I say, 'Why me, what did I do to deserve this?' Help me to remember that you do not punish your creation by bringing disease, but that you are Emmanuel, God with us. You are as close to me as my next breath.

AIDS has caused a separation between the body I knew and my body now. Help me to remember that I am more than my body and, while it pains me greatly to see what has happened to it, I am more than my body. I am part of you and you me.

AIDS has separated me from my family. O God, help me and them to realize that I haven't changed, I'm still their child, our love for each other is your love for us. Help them overcome their fear, embarrassment and guilt. Their love brought me into this world. Help them share as much as possible with me.

AIDS has caused a separation between me and my friends; my friendships have been so important to me. They are especially important now. Help me, O God, to recognize their fear, and help them to realize my increasing need for them to love in any way they can.

AIDS has separated me from my society, my work world and my community. It pains me for them to see me differently now. Forgive them for allowing their ignorance of this disease and their fear to blind their judgements. Help me with my anger towards them.

AIDS has caused a separation between me and my Church. Help the Church to restore its ministry to 'the least of these' by reaching out to me and others. Help them suspend their judgements and love me as they have before. Help me and them to realize that the Church is the Body of Christ, that separation and alienation wound the body.

God of our birth and God of our death, help us know you have been, you are, and you are to come. Amen.

(anonymous)

5. O God, today as we focus on HIV and AIDS, we confront things we would often prefer to avoid.

Here we are confronted with chaos.

Here we feel the surging Spirit of God who shakes our foundations and hurls the mountains into the sea; we feel the God who upsets our order and threatens our security. *Kyrie eleison* ('Lord have mercy').

Here we are confronted with death.

Here we face the truth that we are vulnerable and mortal; here we face the fact that life is fragile and precious; here we face the challenge that we cannot come to terms with our life, until we have first come to terms with our death. *Kyrie eleison.*

Here we are confronted with sexuality.

Here we discover that humanity and sexuality are inseparable; and in Jesus Christ we discover that divinity and carnality are inseparable; here we discover that in him our sexuality is redeemed and not denied. *Kyrie eleison.*

Here we are confronted with judgement.

Here we stand before the judgement of God that rejects our self-righteousness; that tears away our efforts to justify ourselves; that condemns our efforts to find acceptance by condemning others. *Kyrie eleison.*

Here we are confronted with fear.

Here we face the fear of those who are different from us; here we face the fear of chaos and death; of sexuality and judgement. *Kyrie eleison.*

Here we are confronted with grace.

Here we feel the embrace of God's grace that accepts and affirms, that is faithful and merciful. Loving God, redeem us from captivity and turn our fears to freedom. Be with us today and bless us, in Jesus' name. Amen.

(Lance Stone)

6.   Blessed are you, God of life, for in Jesus, the servant of all, we see your human face. We give thanks for the good news of healing and liberation which is preached to the whole world by those who live with HIV or AIDS. We pray that in the midst of this world, and before the eyes of all people with whom we are united through our common humanity, we may listen to their words so as to become more aware of their needs. May we recognize that as one part of the body is gifted with life and healing, so also is the whole. Then, may we proclaim our hope in the coming of your reign when all will be one in a new humanity, and you will be all in all, God, for ever and ever.

(Martin Pendergast)

The Blessing of Oil for Anointing

1.   Blessed are you, eternal God,
     Source of all healing,
     you have given us the means

by which you make your creatures whole,
our presence and our skills,
our understanding of your laws
and our humility before the unknown,
our words and our hands,
medicines that soothe and cure,
machines that aid our work.
We give ourselves to you:
empty us of all that hinders the flow
of your healing Spirit.
Take our hands and our lives
that we may live in your image
and reflect your glory.

In the name of God,
who is great and good and love,
in the name of God,
giving life, bearing pain, making whole:
by the laying on of these hands
may the healing Spirit bless and support you,
for you are dearly loved;
by the laying on of these hands
may the healing Spirit flow freely in you and through
     you,
the power that is waiting to be set free among us,
that seeks our will and consent and trust;
by the laying on of these hands
may the healing Spirit confirm us in our faith,
making us strong together as one Body
in the service and friendship of Christ.
N, through the laying on of these hands
and through our prayer,
receive the gift of the healing Spirit of God.

N, may the Holy Spirit,
the Giver of Life and Healing,
fill you with Light and Love,
and make you whole;
through Jesus Christ our Saviour.

(Jim Cotter)

2.   God of hope and consolation, you sent Jesus as the life of
the world to bring healing for all people. We ask that you would
hear our prayer and send the healing Spirit of Jesus to be with us
through this oil. May it be a soothing balm, bringing the fullness
and richness of the earth from which it came. May this oil bring
your life and healing in body, soul, and spirit to all who are
anointed with it. And may this oil always be a reminder of your
care for us and for all who suffer. For it is in the name of Jesus
that we pray.

(Louis F. Kavar)

3.   Loving and gracious God, send forth your Spirit to brood
and hover over us and this oil. We pray that the sharing of this
oil may be a source of your strength and courage in our fight
against the suffering and injustice of AIDS. May the anointing
with this oil be a symbol of our commitment to serve you in our
brothers and sisters who suffer because of AIDS. And may it be
a healing balm, for our own fear and hurt as we live with AIDS.
We pray this in the Spirit of Jesus, our brother, who was
anointed with oil by the woman to be strengthened for his own
suffering. Amen.

(Louis F. Kavar)

If just the laying on of hands is given the following is said: Jesus
Christ touched people and they were healed. Most of us express
things words cannot through touch. We follow the example of

using touch as a way of communicating the love of God. This celebration of God's love for each of us brings strength, hope and peace.

(Ecumenical AIDS Support Team, Edinburgh)

Remembering the Dead

We gather in remembrance of those whom we have loved and who have died because of AIDS.

We remember with fondness the many gifts they shared with us.

We remember our lovers and spouses with whom we shared so intimately.

We mourn the loss of their gentle touch, the quiet moments which we shared and the love that we celebrated.

We remember our children for whom we had great hopes.

We grieve the loss of their dreams for the future knowing that they have left us all too soon.

We remember our fathers and mothers, brothers and sisters, uncles, aunts and cousins.

Those whose lives we shared from our earliest years, who shaped our lives and character, who gave us part of themselves.

We remember our friends who shared with us in work and leisure.

We remember with fondness the many hours spent in laughter, good times and happiness. We miss the warmth of their presence.

We recall by name all those whom we have lost to AIDS:

Names are called out or a memorial quilt is unfolded.

Loving God, Mother and Father of us all, we remember the gift of life you shared with us through our loved ones who have died. We ask that you hold each of them close to yourself and fulfil in yourself all of their hopes and dreams. Be with us in our loss. Send your good Spirit to hover over us, gently touching our pain. Fill the empty spaces of our lives with your loving presence. And bring us into full union with you and those whom we love.

Amen.

(Louis F. Kavar)

Final Prayers And Blessings

1.   Lord Jesus Christ, you stretched your arms out in love on the hard wood of the cross that all might come within your saving embrace: Strengthen all who bear heavy burdens, refresh the weary, cheer the sad, cherish the loveless and grant your peace and joy to all.

Amen.

(Ecumenical AIDS Support Team, Edinburgh)

2.   Receive a blessing
      for all that may be required of you,
      that love may drive out fear,

that you may be more perfectly
abandoned to the will of God,
and that peace and contentment
may reign in your hearts,
and through you may spread
over the face of the earth.
The blessing of God,
Giver of Life,
Bearer of Pain,
Maker of Love,
Creator and Sustainer,
Liberator and Redeemer,
Healer and Sanctifier,
be with you
and all whom you love,
both living and departed,
now and for ever. Amen.

(Jim Cotter)

3.   Know that as certain as night follows day and day follows
night, God's faithfulness will be with us each moment of our
lives. Even if we are unfaithful, God still remains faithful, for God
cannot deny the very God-self in whose image we have been
created.

(Louis F. Kavar)

4.   Having been strengthened and assured by God's presence
and our sharing with each other, let us go forth this day to live
boldly and with courage in the face of AIDS. May we dispel all
fear with the surety of our faith and hope.

Amen.

(Louis F. Kavar)

5.   The heritage of God's kingdom is prepared for you and for all people who seek the Lord and serve him where he has declared his presence, especially amongst those in need. I invite you now to declare your readiness to serve Christ in the many faces of AIDS.

We promise to serve the Lord in all who are considered the least of his brothers and sisters, so that sharing his poverty and suffering, we may also share his glory.

May almighty God bless you, the Father, the Son and the Holy Spirit.

Amen.

(Catholic AIDS Link)

Readings

1.   I will not restrain my mouth; I will speak in the anguish of my spirit; I will complain in the bitterness of my soul . . . When I say 'My bed will comfort me, my couch will ease my complaint,' then you scare me with dreams and visions, so that I would choose strangling and death rather than this body. I loathe my life; I would not live forever. Let me alone, for my days are a breath. What are human beings, that you make so much of them, that you set your mind on them, visit them every morning, test them every moment? Will you not look away from me for a while, let me alone until I swallow my spittle? If I sin, what do I do to you, you watcher of humanity? Why have you made me your target? Why have I become a burden to you? Why do you not pardon my transgression and take away my iniquity? For

now I shall lie in the earth; you will seek me, but I shall not be.

(Job 7.11, 13–21)

2. But now thus says the Lord ... Do not fear, for I have redeemed you; I have called you by name, you are mine. When you pass through the waters, I will be with you; and through the rivers, they shall not overwhelm you; when you walk through fire you shall not be burned, and the flame shall not consume you. For I am the Lord your God, the Holy One of Israel, your Saviour.

(Isaiah 43.1–3*a*)

3. [Jesus said] Come to me, all you that are weary and are carrying heavy burdens, and I will give you rest. Take my yoke upon you, and learn from me; for I am gentle and humble of heart, and you will find rest for your souls. For my yoke is easy, and my burden is light.

(Matthew 11.28–30)

4. So do not lose heart. Even though our outer nature is wasting away, our inner nature is being renewed day by day. For this slight momentary affliction is preparing us for an eternal weight of glory beyond all measure, because we look not at what can be seen but at what cannot be seen; for what can be seen is temporary, but what cannot be seen is eternal.

(2 Corinthians 4.17–18)

5. At this time in history, when our common body is broken so badly by AIDS and by violence, we are likely to find ourselves wrestling with the spectre of death. Death is a passage – into what, we are not sure. But I am confident that the irrepressible love of God, the sacred power of the erotic, does not simply leave us behind at our death. An experience of undying friendship

can provide the basis of an eschatology: of how we experience endings.

Closure, termination, and death can be cruel and harsh, unjust and unwelcome. In friendship, however, the end is not final. Friends bear one another up here and now and well into eternity, the realm outside of time as we measure it. This bearing up of one another, the capacity for undying friendship, is our passion: It is what we suffer and celebrate together; it is what we are willing to die for, hence, what we are able to live for. It secures our lovemaking as well as our leavetaking in faith that our story is not over.

(Carter Heyward)

6.   Beyond the movements of [three men at a busy airport] stands the dark figure of the bishop. They are men in their forties, like him. Nothing very special about them, except that they are dressed as some gay men do. From their talking two are English and one American. The American does not look very well. Thin and grey in the face, his leather jacket hanging loose from his shoulders . . . The three are saying goodbye. They are standing close together, arms about each other in an embrace and a hug. From time to time one will kiss the other and pat his back. One of them brushes away tears with the back of his hand, suddenly laughing at his own emotions, a little embarrassed perhaps . . .

A discreet man, [the bishop] does not want to stare too pointedly. His eyes slide towards the three, then quickly look away. His fingers tighten round the beads as he jerks them a little quicker. He does not like what he has seen. Then his eyes are back again, suspicious, and he catches a trinitarian hug. He frowns disapproval, shaking his head. He turns away in a scowl of disgust, of terror, but in his own mind he cannot leave them alone . . . For me the bishop and the three friends are pictures of how we envision God. Two manifestations of divinity. The bishop's God is somewhere over the rainbow, way up high. He is distant, unapproachable, unengaged in human affairs except as the God of controlling power, looking down on us, watching us, watching our mistakes . . . With this God there is no satisfaction and no delight, but always disapproval . . .

The three friends signal that love, not hatred, is the heart of God. In their support and care of one another they say to me: God is our friend and not our enemy. In their touch and in their mutuality they say that God is with us. God is by us. We can know God. Know God not only in an intellectual sense, but in the deep and intimate, sensate ways we come to know a lover or a friend. In our lovings and our friendship we can come to know God in what we experience. We can encounter God as the God who loves in those who cherish us, who loves in those we cherish. This is the God of the three; not a distant disapproving God, but a God who is close, who supports and strengthens and stands with us. God who challenges us to become whatever is most beautiful and excellent in us. God who nurses all that is most hurting in us. God, confronting all that is most hurtful in us. God who is nearby, strengthening, encouraging. When we stand together, when we love one another, it is then that we know this God.

(Mark Pryce)

7.   It is a time of fear, of apprehension,
        a fear of pain and disfigurement,
        a fear of hateful eyes and deeds of violence,
        a fear of the power of those who want
        to quarantine, to imprison,
        to tattoo with identity marks
        (shades of Auschwitz),
        a fear of the death-dealing.
        There is a tightening,

a pressure on the chest,
a desire for air, for space
beyond the narrow constricted gate.
There is cold fear in a time of tribulation,
a time of the olive press, the winepress,
the crushing of the grapes,
and no guarantee of a good vintage ...
Again arises from the heart of suffering the ancient cry,
O God, why? O God, how long?
And the cry is met with silence.
Dare I look steadily at Christ,
at God involved in the isolation and despair,
willing to be contaminated, to be infected,
loving faithfully and in patient endurance,
until all that is being created reaches its final destiny,
in glory, joy, and love?
And yet, why *this* degree of pain?
Why these ever-repeated battles,
with a swathe cut through a generation?
Horrific sacrifice – for what?

(Jim Cotter)

8.   In the early sixteenth century, the artist Grunewald painted
an altarpiece depicting the crucifixion. The torn, lacerated body
of Christ is also covered in hundreds of sores, sores that obviously
add to the agony of the dying Christ. In those days central
Europe was wracked by a disease that caused death, that caused
those around to recoil in fear. The sores on the body of
Grunewald's Christ were the syphilitic sores of Christ's suffering
humanity. The symbolism is clear: the body of Christ, the
Church, suffered from the scourges of the world, and at that
moment the scourge was a sexually transmitted, deadly disease
for which in that moment of time there was no cure.

Today, some four hundred and fifty years later, the body of Christ is suffering. The body of Christ is suffering because the people of God are suffering. And once again the suffering is from disease and fear. The disease is AIDS and HIV, and the fear is just as irrational now as it was in the sixteenth century. We are all vulnerable, for we, though many, are one body. We are all powerful, for we have the power to lift up those who are burdened. It is we who are called to embrace, to hold, enfold, to kiss as sisters and brothers in Christ, the thousands of women, men and children, who bear in their bodies this further mark of our fallenness. We are the body of Christ, seeking to be a community of comfort and support, and a Church of help and hope.

Today, we must declare anew the marks of the Church, the marks of the body of Christ. Love, pardon, union, faith, hope, light and joy — these are the new marks of the body to which we belong, new marks of the new and risen body of Christ, new marks which will cover and heal the marks of disease, new marks for us to show to all the world.

(anonymous)

6

The Death of Friends

It is a well-known fact that we live in a culture that attempts to deny the reality of death. Discussion of death and dying in everyday life is discouraged and labelled as 'morbid', and when death occurs everything is done to sanitize it and remove it from view. The bereaved are discouraged from talking about their loss or displaying their grief and pressure is put upon them to return to 'normal' as soon as possible; life has to go on as if nothing has happened. Yet the medical and psychological evidence suggests that this approach to death is decidedly unhealthy for all concerned. In order to be whole, healthy human beings we need to allow ourselves time to mourn our loss. We need to let go of our fear of mortality. Christianity should be able to help here, holding up as it does a God who experienced what it means to be human and who has known the terror of death, the despair of grief and the feelings of apparent meaninglessness that death induces. Christianity also offers the hope that death is not the last word, that beyond death is the possibility of new life, new relationship, new being – a foretaste of which can be experienced in this life, if we let go of the fear of chaos, lack of control and meaninglessness which underlies our fear of death.

Death of course shares the distinction of being 'the great taboo' with sexuality in general and homosexuality in particular. When a gay or lesbian person dies, in whatever circumstances, a great deal of additional pain can result. In most funeral services

the focus is on the deceased as heterosexual family member —
wife/husband, daughter/son, sister/brother etc. — and the only
people given permission and support to grieve are those related
to that person by blood or marriage. When a gay or lesbian
person dies the danger is that (often for the best of motives)
during funeral or memorial services their sexuality and their
relationships will not be acknowledged in the prayers, readings
or minister's words. Partner and friends may even be excluded
from the services, with the result that the funeral becomes a farce,
a lie, and persons in the deceased's life (who may have been
much more significant than blood relatives) are not given the
chance to say goodbye and give thanks for their friend. The true
family is excluded.

The same dangers exist when the deceased's primary relation
ship has been with a friend, although not expressed sexually, or
when friends have been closer than the family to the deceased.
Alternatively, when a young adult dies, their friends who may
have had little contact with the person's family before the death
may feel uncomfortable at the funeral, not wanting to trespass on
the family's grief but feeling that the person they knew was
somehow different to the son/daughter being mourned there.
When this happens the friends may need to create a space in
which they can come together and mourn their loss.

It is to help name the truth in circumstances such as these that
I have collected together material for use in funerals and memorial
services. At such a difficult time few would want to create a
completely new service. The material in this section could easily
be incorporated into the funeral services of the main Christian
denominations which tend to follow a similar pattern. The fire or
candle-lighting ceremony attempts to symbolize the truth that
friendship can survive even death and that a friend's memory can
continue to encourage, support, sustain and inspire us. Part one
can take place after the opening hymn or sentences from scripture.

The introductions can replace or be incorporated into the introductory prayers. The readings, prayers and final blessings can be used to supplement or replace those found in the service book. Part two of the fire or candle-lighting ceremony could take place during the final hymn at a church service or at the grave or after the committal at the crematorium. Those who do wish to create a funeral or memorial service – friends who are excluded from a funeral may like to hold their own memorial service for the deceased in order to say goodbye – can also draw upon this material, perhaps creating other ceremonies which help to express their affection for their dead friend and their grief at their loss, such as playing some of the friend's favourite music; placing a large photograph of the person at the centre of the gathering and placing a lighted candle in front of it as people share their memories; planting a tree in the person's memory. It is extremely important to come together as friends, for in grief we need others, particularly if our right to grieve is being denied. But the material in this section can also be used for private meditation, for those moments when we are alone and grief overwhelms us.

For those wanting to create their own funeral services, ironically the best and most practical guide I know is *Funerals without God*, published by the British Humanist Association. The Gay Bereavement Project offers a counselling and support service for gay and lesbian people and there are a number of organizations such as Cruse and the National Association of Bereavement Services that will offer similar services to all regardless of sexuality. The addresses of all these organizations are to be found at the end of the book.

Fire or Candle-lighting Ceremony: Part One

The leader lights a small fire or candle, saying: Jesus said, 'I am the light of the world. Whoever follows me will never walk in darkness but will have the light of life.' Let us remember that all the darkness in the world has not put out a single light.

(Dudley Cave)

Introductions

1. We meet today with sorrow in our hearts. We meet also in thankfulness. We come with grief because one we love is no more among us. We come also in gratitude, in praise, in tribute to the life of N.

We come in sorrow, confronting the fact that life ends. This is a condition of our birth, that at the end of the road, near or far, stands always our death. All the generations have had to bear this heavy truth.

The need that is upon us is the need to accept both the glory and the tragedy of life, its holiness and its limits.

The love of the human heart is the most real and the most beautiful of all the realities we know. It is the richest gift we have. It is the love that joins us together as lovers, as husband and wife, as father and mother, parent and child, and as friends and neighbours. Whatever the length of time may be, to have known something of this is to have experienced the supreme privilege of being human.

The anguish of parting cannot destroy this most real of all

realities. The love has been, the affection has existed, the ties
have been woven, life has been shared, the joys and the sorrows.
This has been as real and strong as anything in life. The love that
was once born can never die, for it has become part of our life
woven into every texture of our being.

So here and now we bear witness to the N we knew in life
who, now in death, bequeaths a subtle part, precious and loved,
which will be with us in truth and beauty, in dignity and courage
and love to the end of our days.

(Dudley Cave)

2.   We have come together and to this place today to say
goodbye to our friend, N, who died on . . . to remember the good
and bad times we shared with him/her and to give thanks for a life
that enriched ours. Memorial services are extremely important to
our community, for they are an opportunity for friends to say
goodbye and to acknowledge their grief at the loss of one who
was held dear. When a person dies the focus of attention tends to
fall upon the immediate family and little space is created for
friends to grieve. But we know that friendships often mean as
much as family relationships, sometimes more, and it is right and
proper to create a space to celebrate our friendship with N and
mourn its passing. Like the female friends of Jesus who went early
in the day to mourn privately at his tomb, we come here today
and we hear the same words spoken about our friend as were said
about Jesus that day. 'Do not be afraid . . . He/she is not here . . .
he/she is going ahead of you . . . there you will see him/her again.'

(Elizabeth Stuart)

3.   Hear the words of the prophet Jeremiah: The sound of
mourning and bitter weeping is heard! Rachel mourns her children, refusing to be comforted because her children are no
more!

Like Rachel, we mourn the loss of our loved one. We grieve his/her loss, longing to share with them once again.

And Jesus said: Blessed are they who mourn, for they shall be comforted. As we gather for this time of worship, we seek comfort in our loss. Come, Holy Spirit, send your cool breeze to ease the pain of our grieving hearts.

(Louis F. Kavar)

Prayers

1. Let us remember those who are most keenly conscious of loss today, N and N . . . and all N's (the deceased) friends. May they find consolation in a gratitude for all that N (the deceased) has meant to them and to others.

We hold in our minds the needs and sorrows of others as well as our own needs and sorrows, seeking that we may know the places we may serve and how best to do the right thing at the right time.

We would learn to accept even the hard and bitter things we have known and suffered, the mysteries of pain, of sickness and of death. May we gain from them a truer sense of direction for the days ahead.

We would fashion from our grief and sadness a song of praise to the goodness of life, that our love for N may be witnessed, renewed and strengthened in our love for others.

So may we be part of the world's light and not its darkness, its faith and not its fear, its love and not its hate, so we may know in new and deeper ways that we are members one of another. Let the horizon of our minds include the great family here on earth with us; those who have gone before and left to us the heritage of their memory shaped by their work; and those whose lives will be shaped by what we do or leave undone.

Amen.

(Dudley Cave)

2.   The God of peace sanctify you completely,
       even to the glory of the great day:
       faithful is the God who calls,
       the God whose promises will be fulfilled.
       N,
       God bless you richly,
       grow in grace,
       make love,
       keep us in loving mind,
       hold us close in the Presence,
       guide us,
       pray for us.

(Jim Cotter)

3.   Great God of Jesus Christ, we know that for you in death, life is changed, not ended. Despite our faith in the promise of new life, the changes brought about by the death of N cause us grief and pain, loneliness and depression, anger and emptiness.

As Jesus wept at the tomb of Lazarus, so we weep because of our own loss. As the disciples on the road to Emmaus were numb and in shock because of Jesus' death, so we too have found times when we wander aimlessly beside ourselves with grief. As the apostles huddled in fear behind locked doors after Jesus' death, so we too are afraid of many things because of the loss of N.

Be with us at this time. Support us through all the confusing feelings we experience in our grief and mourning. Enable us to be patient with ourselves when the pain returns. And confirm within us a living faith in your abiding presence which will always be with us, today and forever.

Amen.

(Louis F. Kavar)

4. We commit you to the keeping of Mother Earth which bears us all. We are glad that you lived, that we saw your face, knew your friendship, and walked the way of life with you. We deeply cherish the memory of your words and deeds and character. We leave you in peace. With respect we bid you farewell. In love we remember your companionship, your kindly ways. And thinking of you in this manner, let us go on in quietness of spirit and life in friendship one with another.

(Andrew Hill)

5. Give rest, O Christ, to your servant with your saints,
    where sorrow and pain are no more,
    neither sighing, but life everlasting.
    Creator and Maker of humankind, you only are immortal,
    and we are mortal, formed of the earth,
    and to the earth we shall return:
    for so you did ordain when you created us, saying,
    Dust thou art and unto dust thou shalt return.

    **All we go down to the dust,
    and, weeping o'er the grave, we make our song:
    Alleluia, alleluia, alleluia.
    Give rest, O Christ, to your servant with your saints,
    where sorrow and pain are no more,
    neither sighing, but life everlasting.**

(Jim Cotter)

Final Blessings

1. Go into the world this day being strengthened by the memories of joy and laughter you have shared with N. Live courageously, for it is the presence of the living God which sustains you now and always.

(Louis F. Kavar)

2. Blessed are we who mourn for we have been privileged to walk alongside N through life's journey.

Blessed are we who mourn for we have been graced with the precious gift of N's friendship.

Blessed are we who mourn for we entrust N body and soul to the God who bursts the bonds of death.

Blessed are we who mourn, for in return God entrusts to us the vision of the divine commonwealth in which every tear will be wiped away and death will be no more, mourning and crying and pain will be no more. We go from here to take up the challenge of transforming vision into reality, comforted and inspired by the memory of N.

God gives and God takes away. Blessed be the name of God.

(Elizabeth Stuart)

3. May the God of the exodus who goes before us always welcome you, N, into the glory of the resurrection. And may God bless us, your mourners, with the strength to continue our pilgrimage as we each seek the place of our resurrection.

(Elizabeth Stuart)

Fire or Candle-lighting Ceremony: Part Two

The mourners light a candle from the fire or candle lit at the beginning of the service to carry out with them, as a sign that they take something of the deceased with them back into their lives. The fire or central candle is then put out.

Readings

1. David intoned this lamentation over Saul and his son
   Jonathan . . .
   Your glory, O Israel, lies slain upon your high places!
   How the mighty have fallen! . . .
   Saul and Jonathan, beloved and lovely!
   In life and in death they were not divided;
   they were swifter than eagles,
   they were stronger than lions . . .
   How the mighty have fallen
   in the midst of the battle! . . .
   I am distressed for you, my brother Jonathan;
   greatly beloved were you to me;
   your love to me was wonderful,
   passing the love of women.
                     (2 Samuel 1.17, 19, 23, 25a, 26)

2. Then the Lord God will wipe away the tears from all faces, and the disgrace of his people he will take away from all the earth, for the Lord has spoken. It will be said on that day, Lo, this is our God: we have waited for him, so that he might save us.

This is the Lord for whom we have waited; let us be glad and rejoice in his salvation.

(Isaiah 25.8–9)

3.   The steadfast love of the Lord never ceases, his mercies never come to an end; they are new every morning; great is your faithfulness. 'The Lord is my portion,' says my soul, 'therefore I will hope in him.' The Lord is good to those who wait for him, to the soul that seeks him. It is good that one should wait quietly for the salvation of the Lord. . . . For the Lord will not reject forever. Although he causes grief, he will have compassion according to the abundance of his steadfast love; for he does not willingly afflict or grieve anyone.

(Lamentations 3.22–6, 31–3)

4.   Thus says the Lord God: 'I am going to open your graves, and bring you up from your graves, O my people; and I will bring you back to the land of Israel. And you shall know that I am the Lord, when I open your graves, and bring you up from your graves, O my people. I will put my spirit within you, and you shall live, and I will place you on your own soil; then you shall know that I, the Lord, have spoken and will act,' says the Lord.

(Ezekiel 37.12–14)

5.   When Jesus arrived, he found that Lazarus had already been in the tomb four days. Now, Bethany was near Jerusalem, some two miles away, and many of the Jews had come to Martha and Mary to console them about their brother. When Martha heard that Jesus was coming, she went and met him, while Mary stayed at home. Martha said to Jesus, 'Lord, if you had been here, my brother would not have died. But even now I know that God will give you whatever you ask of him.' Jesus said to her, 'Your

brother will rise again.' Martha said to him, 'I know that he will rise again in the resurrection on the last day.' Jesus said to her, 'I am the resurrection and the life. Those who believe in me will never die. Do you believe this?'

(John 11.17–26)

6. When Mary came where Jesus was and saw him, she knelt at his feet and said to him, 'Lord, if you had been here, my brother would not have died.' When Jesus saw her weeping, and the Jews who came with her also weeping, he was greatly disturbed in spirit and deeply moved. He said, 'Where have you laid him?' They said to him, 'Lord, come and see.' Jesus began to weep. So the Jews said, 'See how he loved him!' But some of them said, 'Could not he who opened the eyes of the blind man have kept this man from dying?'

Then Jesus, again greatly disturbed, came to the tomb. It was a cave, and a stone was lying against it. Jesus said, 'Take away the stone.' Martha, the sister of the dead man, said to him, 'Lord, already there is a stench because he has been dead four days.' Jesus said to her, 'Did I not tell you that if you believed, you would see the glory of God?' So they took away the stone. And Jesus looked upward and said, 'Father, I thank you for having heard me. I knew that you always hear me, but I have said this for the sake of the crowd standing here, so that they may believe that you sent me.' When he had said this, he cried with a loud voice, 'Lazarus, come out!' The dead man came out, his hands and feet bound with strips of cloth, and his face wrapped in a cloth. Jesus said to them, 'Unbind him, and let him go.'

(John 11.32–44)

7. For I am convinced that neither death, nor life, nor angels, nor rulers, nor things present, nor things to come, nor powers, nor height, nor depth, nor anything else in all creation, will

be able to separate us from the love of God in Christ Jesus our
Lord.

(Romans 8.38–9)

8.   Then I saw a new heaven and a new earth; for the first
heaven and the first earth had passed away, and the sea was no
more. And I saw the holy city, the new Jerusalem, coming down
out of heaven from God, prepared as a bride adorned for her
husband. And I heard a loud voice from the throne saying,

> See, the home of God is among mortals.
> He will dwell with them as their God;
> they will be his peoples,
> and God himself will be with them;
> he will wipe away every tear from their eyes.
> Death will be no more;
> mourning and crying and pain will be no more,
> for the first things have passed away.

(Revelation 21.1–4)

9.   She whom we love
     and lose
     is no longer
     where she was before.
     She is now
     wherever we are.

(St John Chrysostom)

10.   A thousand years, you said,
      as our hearts melted.
      I look at the hand you held,
      and the ache is hard to bear.

(Lady Heguri)

11.   When sorrow comes, let us accept it simply, as a part of life. Let the heart be open to pain; let it be stretched by it. All the evidence we have says that this is the better way. An open heart never grows bitter. Or if it does, it cannot remain so. In the desolate hour, there is an outcry; a clenching of the hands upon emptiness; a burning pain of bereavement; a weary ache of loss. But anguish, like ecstasy, is not forever. There comes a gentleness, a returning quietness, a restoring stillness. This, too, is a door to life. Here, also, is a deepening of meaning — and it can lead to dedication; a going forward to the triumph of the soul, the conquering of the wilderness. And in the process will come a deepening inward knowledge that in the final reckoning, all is well.

(A. Powell Davies)

12.   Inevitably our anguish frames the question 'Why?' if not on our lips, then in our hearts. There is no answer that removes this question — no answer that can bridge the chasm of irreparable separation. Life will never be the same, and this is as it should be, for our loved ones are not expendable.

We can meet such loss only with our grief, that uncontrived mixture of courage, affirmation, and inconsolable desolation. Grief is enough; for in our grief we live an answer, as in the depths love and selfishness conjoin until, if we allow it, love asserts its dominance, and we become more aware of the community of living of which life makes us a part.

(Paul Carnes)

13.   Death is nothing at all. I have only slipped away into the next room. I am I, and you are you. Whatever we were to each other, that we still are. Call me by my old familiar name, speak to me in the easy way which you always used. Put no difference in your tone, wear no forced air of solemnity or sorrow. Laugh as

we always laughed at the little jokes we enjoyed together. Pray, smile, think of me, pray for me. Let my name be ever the household word that it always was, let it be spoken without effect, without the trace of a shadow on it. Life means all that it ever meant. It is the same as it ever was; there is unbroken continuity. Why should I be out of mind because I am out of sight? I am waiting for you, for an interval, somewhere very near, just round the corner. All is well.

(Henry Scott Holland)

14.   The Sanskrit word for widow means 'empty'. The pain we feel when someone we love dies comes from this sense of emptiness. When we love someone deeply, we truly become one with that person. Our love becomes part of our core reality, our very essence. Consequently, with the death of the one we love, we experience a loss of our sense of identity, and the meaning goes out of our relationship with the world. We must redefine who we are and what the world means to us ... We all have an absolute need of companionship and sharing in order to success- fully complete the grieving process. We need a loving community to provide some degree of acceptance and hope and to help us to maintain some contact with the living. We can still hear Jesus' plaintive call to his disciples in the garden of Gethsemane, 'Had you not the strength to keep awake one hour?' (Mark 14.37)

(John McNeill)

The following poems are also offered as suggested readings:

C. Day Lewis, 'His Laughter'; John Donne, 'Death, Be Not Proud'; George Eliot, 'O May I Join the Choir Invisible'; Kahlil Gibran, *The Prophet*, pp. 106–10; Judy Grahn, 'A Funeral'; Thomas Gray, 'If I Should Die'; Christina Rossetti, 'Song' and 'Remember'; Edna St Vincent Millay,

'What's This of Death' and 'Conscientious Objector'; William Shake-speare, 'Fear No More'; Percy Bysshe Shelley, 'He has Outsoared the Shadow of our Night'; Dylan Thomas, 'Do Not Go Gentle into that Good Night'; and Walt Whitman, 'Continuities'.

Funeral Services for Lesbians and Gay Men

Funerals for lesbians and gay men can be a problem for clergy and for secular officiants. The funeral should be a springboard for good grief but can be traumatic for the surviving partner. We have heard of a priest who, at the service, prayed for the forgiveness of the deceased's deviant life-style!

If, like the majority of lesbians and gay men, the partnership is discreet, even secret, and known only to a few friends, the surviving partner will find it hard to speak of the relationship to funeral directors, clergy and the various officials concerned.

An officiant who understands the relationship and does not disapprove of that love is essential, and bereaved partners should be included in the service and not feel excluded in any way. All too often they will be at the back, shrouded in personal grief, away from the sympathy being directed to the blood family at the front.

Where possible the partners should be named at some point in the service, in the eulogy or in the prayers or meditation after the committal. Something like this could be said: 'In their grief we remember those who are most keenly conscious of grief and loss: John and Mary, his parents, his sister Ann and his special friend/partner/companion George. May they find consolation in gratitude for all that Henry has meant to them and to others.' If this is not possible, the officiant should make frequent eye-contact with the partner during the service and make a special point of speaking to and touching them after the service.

Partly because of the condemnation of same-sex love by some self-appointed spokespersons of the Church and because of the inability of religious bodies to understand this semi-invisible minority, many lesbians and gay men have rejected organized religion and, throwing out the baby with the bathwater, have rejected God too. Those bereaved by the death of someone who did not believe in God need a meaningful service at least as much as a devout religious person. Such a service need not be cold, can follow the usual pattern with meditation not prayer, but without reference to God or resurrection and with spaces for believers to insert their devotional thoughts. Believers have needs too.

However, when death strikes, most people look to the Church for the funeral; because it is customary, because they want the funeral to be seemly and, perhaps, because they do not realize that it is not necessary for clergy to officiate.

This probably means that the service will be taken by someone on the clergy rota, someone who did not know the dead person and may not have a chance to discuss the service in any depth with those concerned and may even use the first name without checking that is the one used by family and friends. The service could then be a bad experience and reinforce anti-Church feelings.

Many will have no previous experience of funerals and need to be told what will happen. Some will not know that their 'special tune' can be played and that readings from non-biblical sources can be used. Because of the numbness of bereavement they may not be able to press for what they really want and need to be encouraged to make suggestions.

Sensitivity to language is important. Sexist and heterosexist language can just cause additional distress. After the service, whenever possible, the bereaved partner should be treated as a widow or widower would be, receiving the warmth and sympathy from the mourners and supported by the officiant in this. Handshakes, embraces and hugs have their place after the service.

AIDS has added another dimension to grief at funerals. I have taken two funeral services where the parents learnt in one traumatic telephone call that their son was gay and dying. On top of the grief was the sad knowledge that he had not been able to share the problems of his homosexuality, the joys of his partnerships or the fears of his illness with them.

Parents of homosexual children often feel guilty, some believing that all conditions are due to heredity or environment, nature or nurture. They need to know that there are twins where one is homosexual and the other is not and, although the parents may prefer them both to be heterosexual, there are many people of all ages who are glad to be lesbians or gay men.

There can be serious financial problems. If there is no will, everything owned by the dead partner will go to the next of kin or, if there is none, to the Duchy of Cornwall. There is only one way that a same-sex partner might inherit without a will: if it can be proved that the dead partner provided financial support during life, then some provision may be made.

People who love in secret must mourn alone. They were unable to share their feeling of joy with others and cannot share their sorrow. When their partner dies they will have to cope. Friends may wonder why the death of 'just a flat-mate' is causing so much distress. Sensitive clergy will offer post-funeral support or direct mourners to support agencies where there will be space and permission to grieve.

Dudley Cave
Founder member of the Gay Bereavement Project

Notes, Sources and Acknowledgements

Extracts from the New Revised Standard Version of the Bible, copyright © 1989, are used with permission of Oxford University Press.

The author and publishers are grateful to the copyright owners, acknowledged in the notes on sources below, for their permission to reproduce copyright material.

Introduction

1. John Boswell, *Christianity, Social Tolerance, and Homosexuality: Gay People in Western Europe from the Beginning of the Christian Era to the Fourteenth Century*, University of Chicago Press, 1980, pp. 221–6. Aelred's *Spiritual Friendship* is available through the Cistercian Press, distributed in the UK by Mowbrays.
2. See Gerda Lerner, *The Creation of Patriarchy*, New York, Oxford University Press, 1986, p. 239. From a theological point of view we might say that patriarchy is whatever seeks to deny women the dignity, worth and equality of persons made in the image of God.
3. Boswell, *Christianity, Social Tolerance, and Homosexuality*, pp. 221–6.
4. Alfred Kinsey *et al.*, *Sexual Behaviour in the Human Male*, Philadelphia, Saunders, 1948 and *Sexual Behaviour in the Human Female*, Philadelphia, Saunders, 1953.
5. See, e.g., L. William Countryman, *Dirt, Greed and Sex: Sexual Ethics in the New Testament and their Implications for Today*, London, SCM, 1988; George Edwards, *Gay/Lesbian Liberation: A Biblical Perspective*,

New York, The Pilgrim Press, 1984; Tom Horner, *Jonathan Loved David: Homosexuality in Biblical Times*, Philadelphia, Westminster, 1978; John McNeill, *The Church and the Homosexual*, 3rd edn, Boston, Beacon Press, 1988.

6. Adrienne Rich, 'Twenty-One Love Poems: XIII', from *The Fact of a Door Frame: Poems Selected and New 1950–1984*, New York, W. W. Norton and Co., 1984.

7. Mary Hunt, *Fierce Tenderness: A Feminist Theology of Friendship*, New York, Crossroad, 1991, p. 117.

1. Celebrating Lesbian and Gay Relationships

1. John Shelby Spong, *Living in Sin: A Bishop Rethinks Human Sexuality*, New York, Harper and Row, 1988, pp. 200–201.

2. London, Church House Publishing, December 1991, 4:6.

3. Becky Butler, *Ceremonies of the Heart: Celebrating Lesbian Unions*, Washington, Seal Press, 1990, pp. 4–10.

4. John Boswell, *Christianity, Social Tolerance, and Homosexuality: Gay People in Western Europe from the Beginning of the Christian Era to the Fourteenth Century*, University of Chicago Press, 1980.

5. John Boswell, *Rediscovering Gay History: Archetypes of Gay Love in Christian History*, London, Gay Christian Movement, 1982, p. 18. See below, prayers 8, 9 and 10, and blessing 6.

6. ibid., p. 21.

Sentences from Scripture and Psalms

4. Adapted by the Revd Malcolm Johnson.

7. From Jim Cotter, *By Stony Paths: A Version of Psalms 51–100*, Sheffield, Cairns Publications, 1991, pp. 29–30.

Introductions

1. Adapted from Jim Cotter, *Exploring Lifestyles: An Introduction to the*

Service of Blessing for Gay Couples, London, Gay Christian Movement, 1980, p. 19.
2. Adapted from a service of blessing of a same-sex partnership by the Revd Andrew Hill.
3. Adapted from a service of blessing by Dudley Cave.
4. Adapted from an exchange-of-vows ceremony by the Revd Hazel Barkham.
5. Adapted from Rosemary Radford Ruether, *Women-Church: Theology and Practice of Feminist Liturgical Communities*, San Francisco, Harper and Row, 1986, pp. 196–7. Copyright 1985 by Rosemary Radford Ruether. Reprinted by permission of HarperCollins Publishers.

Prayers

1. Jim Cotter, *Exploring Lifestyles: An Introduction to the Service of Blessing for Gay Couples*, London, Gay Christian Movement, 1980, p. 29.
2. Adapted from a service 'Celebrating our Commitment', authors unknown.
3. ibid.
4. Adapted from *Exploring Lifestyles*, p. 27.
5. ibid., pp. 27–8.
6. Adapted from a service of blessing by Dudley Cave.
7. ibid.
8. From a ceremony of the Greek Church celebrating friendship between two people of the same sex, ninth or tenth century AD; adapted from John Boswell, *Rediscovering Gay History: Archetypes of Gay Love in Christian History*, London, Gay Christian Movement, 1982, p. 19.
9. ibid., pp. 19–20.
10. ibid., p. 20.
11. Adapted from a service of blessing of a same-sex partnership by the Revd Ann Peart.

Declarations and Questions of Hope

1. Adapted from a blessing of a friendship by the Revd Hazel Barkham.
2. Adapted from Jim Cotter, *Exploring Lifestyles: An Introduction to the*

Service of Blessing for Gay Couples, London, Gay Christian Movement, 1980, pp. 20–21.

3. Adapted from a service 'Celebrating our Commitment', authors unknown.
4. Adapted from Terry Kime and Sally Meiser in Becky Butler, *Ceremonies of the Heart: Celebrating Lesbian Unions*, Washington, Seal Press, 1990, p. 196.

Charges to Witnesses

1. Adapted from Jim Cotter, *Exploring Lifestyles: An Introduction to the Service of Blessing for Gay Couples*, London, Gay Christian Movement, 1980, p. 29.
2. Adapted from Terry Kime and Sally Meiser in Becky Butler, *Ceremonies of the Heart: Celebrating Lesbian Unions*, Washington, Seal Press, 1990, pp. 197–8.
3. Adapted from Scott W. Alexander in Unitarian Universalist Association, *Same-Gender Services of Union*, Boston, n.d., p. 3.

Promises

1. Adapted from Terry Kime and Sally Meiser in Becky Butler, *Ceremonies of the Heart: Celebrating Lesbian Unions*, Washington, Seal Press, 1990, p. 197.
2. Adapted from a blessing of a friendship by the Revd Hazel Barkham.
3. Adapted from a Holy Union service at the Metropolitan Community Church of Bournemouth.
4. Jim Cotter, *Prayer at Night: A Book for the Darkness*, Exeter, Cairns Publications, 1988, p. 74.
5. Adapted from *The Alternative Celebrations Catalogue*, ed. Milo Shannon-Thornberry, New York, Pilgrim Press, 1982, by Rosemary Radford Ruether, *Women-Church: Theology and Practice of Feminist Liturgical Communities*, San Francisco, Harper and Row, 1986, p. 196.
6. Adapted from F. Jay Deacon in Unitarian Universalist Association, *Same-Gender Services of Union*, Boston, n.d., p. 7.

Exchange of Rings or Gifts

1. Adapted from Jim Cotter, *Exploring Lifestyles: An Introduction to the Service of Blessing for Gay Couples*, London, Gay Christian Movement, 1980, p. 27.
2. Adapted from a Holy Union service at the Metropolitan Community Church of Bournemouth.
3. Adapted from Marion Hansell and Barbara Hicks in Becky Butler, *Ceremonies of the Heart: Celebrating Lesbian Unions*, Washington, Seal Press, 1990, pp. 154–5.
4. Adapted from Judith Meyer in Unitarian Universalist Association, *Same-Gender Services of Union*, Boston, n.d., p. 3.

Blessings

1. Adapted from Jim Cotter, *Exploring Lifestyles: An Introduction to the Service of Blessing for Gay Couples*, London, Gay Christian Movement, 1980, p. 28.
2. Adapted from a service of blessing based upon the traditional Church of England marriage service by the Revd Malcolm Johnson.
3. Adapted from a service of blessing by Dudley Cave.
4. Adapted from Marion Hansell and Barbara Hicks in Becky Butler, *Ceremonies of the Heart: Celebrating Lesbian Unions*, Washington, Seal Press, 1990, p. 155.
5. Adapted from a service of blessing based upon the traditional Church of England marriage service by the Revd Malcolm Johnson.
6. Adapted from a ceremony from the Greek Church of the ninth or tenth century AD, celebrating friendship between two people of the same sex, in John Boswell, *Rediscovering Gay History: Archetypes of Gay Love in Christian History*, London, Gay Christian Movement, 1982, pp. 20–21.

Candle-lighting Ceremonies

1. Adapted from a service of blessing by Dudley Cave. The candle-lighting ceremony was written by Bruce Marshall.

2. Adapted from a Holy Union service at the Metropolitan Community Church of Bournemouth.
3. Adapted from Rosanne Leipzig and Judy Mable in Becky Butler, *Ceremonies of the Heart: Celebrating Lesbian Unions*, Washington, Seal Press, 1990, p. 300.

Symbols of Communion

1. Adapted from Rose Tillemans, 'Commitment', *Bondings* (a publication of New Ways ministry), Winter 1988–9, p. 4.
2. Adapted from a service of blessing based upon the traditional Church of England marriage service by the Revd Malcolm Johnson.
3. Adapted from Phyllis Athey and Mary Jo Osterman in Rosemary Radford Ruether, *Women-Church: Theology and Practice of Feminist Liturgical Communities*, San Francisco, Harper and Row, 1986, pp. 199–200.
4 Adapted from Rosanne Leipzig and Judy Mable in Becky Butler, *Ceremonies of the Heart: Celebrating Lesbian Unions*, Washington, Seal Press, 1990, p. 299.
5. Adapted from F. Jay Deacon in Unitarian Universalist Association, *Same-Gender Services of Union*, Boston, n.d., pp. 4–5.

Final Blessings

1. Adapted from Universal Fellowship of Metropolitan Community Churches, *Holy Union Resources*, Los Angeles, 1985, p. 4
2. From Phyllis Athey and Mary Jo Osterman in Rosemary Radford Ruether, *Women-Church: Theology and Practice of Feminist Liturgical Communities*, San Francisco, Harper and Row, 1986, p. 200.
3 and 4. From F. Jay Deacon in Unitarian Universalist Association, *Same-Gender Services of Union*, Boston. n.d., p. 5.

Certificates of Contract

1. Adapted from a service of blessing based upon the traditional Church of England marriage service by the Revd Malcolm Johnson.
2. Adapted from a service of blessing of a same-sex partnership by the Revd Ann Peart.

Readings

10. Quoted from Jane Wynne Willson, *To Love and to Cherish: A Guide to Non-Religious Wedding Ceremonies*, London, British Humanist Association, 1988, p. 14.
11. ibid., p. 15.
12. ibid., pp. 28–9.
13. From 'Meditations on Loving in God', in Jim Cotter, *Pleasure, Pain and Passion: Some Perspectives on Sexuality and Spirituality*, Exeter, Cairns Publications, 1988, p. 102.
14. ibid., p. 110.
15. Bill Kirkpatrick, *AIDS: Sharing the Pain: Pastoral Guidelines*, London, Darton, Longman and Todd, 1988, p. 35.
16. Carter Heyward, *Our Passion for Justice: Images of Power, Sexuality and Liberation*, New York, The Pilgrim Press, 1984, p. 93.
17. Atimah, 'Passion', in Becky Butler, *Ceremonies of the Heart: Celebrating Lesbian Unions*, Washington, Seal Press, 1990, p. 287.
18. Quoted by Rosanne Leipzig and Judy Mable in Becky Butler, *Ceremonies of the Heart: Celebrating Lesbian Unions*, Washington, Seal Press, 1990, p. 290.
19. Kahlil Gibran, 'Jesus', quoted in Carl Seaburg, *Great Occasions: Readings for the Celebration of Birth, Coming of Age, Marriage, and Death*, Boston, Skinner House Books, 1968, pp. 93–4. From *Jesus the Son of Man* by Kahlil Gibran, copyright 1928 by Kahlil Gibran and renewed 1956 by Administrators CTA of Kahlil Gibran Estate and Mary G. Gibran. Reprinted by permission of Alfred A. Knopf, Inc.
20. Thomas à Kempis, *The Imitation of Christ*, Harmondsworth, Penguin, 1952, pp. 97–8.

2. Housewarmings

1. Adapted from a housewarming liturgy by the Revd Hazel Barkham.

2. Blessing adapted from the Siddur of Shir Chadash from Sheila Horowitz and Shelley Pearlman in Becky Butler, *Ceremonies of the Heart: Celebrating Lesbian Unions*, Washington, Seal Press, 1990, p. 109.
3. Final Prayer adapted from Rosemary Radford Ruether, *Women-Church: Theology and Practice of Feminist Liturgical Communities*, San Francisco, Harper and Row, 1986, p. 203.

Readings

4. Kahlil Gibran, *The Prophet*, London, Pan Books, 1991 edn, pp. 42–5.

3. A Celebration of Coming Out

Introductions

1. Adapted from a liturgy by the Revd Rebecca Parker and the Revd Joanne Brown, in Rosemary Radford Ruether, *Women-Church: Theology and Practice of Feminist Liturgical Communities*, Harper and Row, San Francisco, 1986, pp. 173–4.

Prayers

1. Chris Glaser, *Coming out to God: Prayers for Lesbians and Gay Men, their Families and Friends*, Louisville, Westminster/John Knox Press, 1991, pp. 86–7.
2. The Revd Rebecca Parker and the Revd Joanne Brown, in Rosemary Radford Ruether, *Women-Church: Theology and Practice of Feminist Liturgical Communities*, San Francisco, Harper and Row, 1986, p. 177.
3. Radclyffe Hall, *The Well of Loneliness*, London, Virago, 1982 edn, p. 447.

Readings

2. Elizabeth Stuart, 'Coming Out of the Tomb', from a meditation written for Lesbian and Gay Christian Movement, Roman Catholic Caucus Newsletter, 1990.
3. Carter Heyward, *Our Passion for Justice: Images of Power, Sexuality and Liberation*, New York, The Pilgrim Press, 1984, pp. 81–2.
4. Matthew Fox, 'The Spiritual Journey of the Homosexual . . . and Just About Everyone Else', in *A Challenge to Love*, ed. by Robert Nugent, New York, Crossroad, 1983, p. 198.
5. Rita Mae Brown, 'Sappho's Reply', *Lesbian Poetry: An Anthology*, ed. Elly Bulkin and Joan Larkin, Watertown, MA, Persephone Press, 1981, p. 136.

4. Partings

1. Robin Green, *Only Connect: Worship and Liturgy from the Perspective of Pastoral Care*, London, Darton, Longman and Todd, 1987, p. 60.

Introduction

1. Adapted from the *Ritual of Divorce* by Florence Perrella Hayes in Rosemary Radford Ruether, *Women-Church: Theology and Practice of Feminist Liturgical Communities*, San Francisco, Harper and Row, 1986, p. 164.

Rituals and Pronouncement of Separation

1. Adapted from 'A Rite of Divorce' by Rudolph W. Nemser, in Carl Seaburg, *Great Occasions: Readings for the Celebration of Birth, Coming-of-Age, Marriage and Death*, Boston, Beacon Press, 1968. pp. 415, 416; copyright © Rudolph W. Nemser, 1966.

Final Prayer and Blessing

1. From Janet Morley, *All Desires Known*, London, Movement for the Ordination of Women, 1988, p. 28.

Readings

3. Jim Cotter, 'Meditation on Loving in God', *Pleasure, Pain and Passion: Some Perspectives on Sexuality and Spirituality*, Exeter, Cairns Publication, 1988, p. 107.
4. Rebecca Lewin, 'The Lesbian Divorce', from Christian McEwen, *Naming the Waves: Contemporary Lesbian Poetry*, London, Virago, 1988, pp. 117–18.
5. Cited by Harvey Gillman in *The Dunblane Papers: Pastoral Approaches to Lesbian and Gay People*, ed. by Elaine Willis and Ian Dunn, London, Institute for the Study of Christianity and Sexuality, 1990, p. 38.
6. Jean Vanier, *The Broken Body: Journey to Wholeness*, London, Darton, Longman and Todd, 1988, p. 106.

5. Healing Liturgies for People Living with HIV and AIDS

Calls to Worship

1. From a service for hope in the face of AIDS and from a general service concerning AIDS, by Louis F. Kavar, *Liturgical Resources for Worshiping Communities Living with AIDS*, the Mid-Atlantic District of the Universal Fellowship of Metropolitan Community Churches, Gaithersburg, 1989, p. 12. Acknowledgement to Chi Rho Press.
2. ibid., pp. 7–8.

The Lighting of Candles

From an inter-faith celebration of love held at St Martin in the Fields church, London, May 1990.

Prayers

1. Catholic AIDS Link Newsletter, October 1990.
2. From a vigil of hope written by the Ecumenical AIDS Support Team, Edinburgh, 1990.
3. From a service for hope in the face of AIDS, *Liturgical Resources for Worshiping Communities Living with AIDS*, Gaithersburg, 1989. Acknowledgement to Chi Rho Press.
4. Adapted from Bill Kirkpatrick, *AIDS: Sharing the Pain: Pastoral Guidelines*, London, Darton, Longman and Todd, 1988, pp. 110–11.
5. Lance Stone in Sebastian Sandys, *Embracing the Mystery: Prayerful Responses to AIDS*, London, SPCK, 1992, pp. 52–4.
6. Martin Pendergast in ibid., pp. 46–7.

The Blessing of Oil for Anointing

1. Jim Cotter, *Healing – More or Less*, Sheffield, Cairns Publications, 1987, p. 55.
2. From a service for healing, *Liturgical Resources for Worshiping Communities Living with AIDS*, Gaithersburg, 1989, p. 16. Acknowledgement to Chi Rho Press.
3. ibid., p. 19.

Remembering the Dead

From a communal memorial service, ibid., pp. 24–5.

Final Prayers and Blessings

1. The Ecumenical AIDS Support Team, Edinburgh.
2. Jim Cotter, *Healing – More or Less*, Sheffield, Cairns Publications, 1987, p. 64.
3. From a service for hope in the face of AIDS, *Liturgical Resources for Worshiping Communities Living with AIDS*, p. 13. Acknowledgement to Chi Rho Press.
4. ibid., p. 19.
5. Catholic AIDS Link Newsletter, October 1990.

Readings

5. Carter Heyward, *Touching Our Strength: The Erotic as Power and the Love of God*, San Francisco, Harper and Row, 1989, p. 138.
6. Extracts from Mark Pryce, 'New Showings: God Revealed in Friendship', in James Woodward, *Embracing the Chaos: Theological Responses to AIDS*, London, SPCK, 1990, pp. 48–52.
7. Jim Cotter, 'Alas Yet More: In a Time of Life-Threatening Epidemic', in *Healing – More or Less*, Sheffield, Cairns Publications, 1987, p. 15.
8. Printed in Catholic AIDS Link Newsletter, October 1990.

6. The Death of Friends

Fire or Candle-lighting Ceremony: Part One

Adapted from a funeral service written by Dudley Cave.

Introductions

1. From a funeral service written by Dudley Cave.
3. Adapted from a service for a grieving community in Louis F. Kavar,

Liturgical Resources for Worshiping Communities Living with AIDS, Mid-Atlantic District of the Universal Fellowship of Metropolitan Community Churches, Gaithersburg, 1989, p. 20. Acknowledgement to Chi Rho Press.

Prayers

1. From a funeral service written by Dudley Cave.
2. Adapted from Jim Cotter, *Prayer in the Morning: A Book for the Day's Beginning*, Sheffield, Cairns Publications, 1989, p. 123.
3. Adapted from a service for a grieving community in *Liturgical Resources for Worshiping Communities Living with AIDS*, Gaithersburg, 1989, pp. 20–21. Acknowledgement to Chi Rho Press.
4. By the Revd Andrew Hill.
5. Adapted from Jim Cotter, op. cit., p. 120.

Final Blessings

1. Adapted from a communal memorial service in *Liturgical Resources for Worshiping Communities Living with AIDS*, Gaithersburg, 1989, p. 26. Acknowledgement to Chi Rho Press.

Readings

10. Lady Heguri, 'A Thousand Years', from Alison Webster, *Just Love: A Resource Book Exploring the Theology of Sexuality*, London, SCM, 1989, p. 27.
11. From Carl Seaburg, *Great Occasions: Readings for the Celebration of Birth, Coming of Age, Marriage, and Death*, Boston, Beacon Press, 1968, pp. 196–7.
12. ibid., p. 197.
14. John J. McNeill, *Taking a Chance on God: Liberating Theology for Gays, Lesbians, and their Lovers, Families, and Friends*, Boston, Beacon Press, 1988, pp. 170–71.

Useful Organizations

United Kingdom

The British Humanist Association, 14 Lamb's Conduit Passage, London WC1R 4RH. Tel: 071 430 0908

CARA (Care and Resources for People Affected by HIV/AIDS), The Basement, 178 Lancaster Road, London W11 1QU. Tel: 071 792 8299

Catholic AIDS Link, PO Box 646, London E6 6QP.

Cruse-Bereavement Care, tel: 081 940 4818.

The Gay Bereavement Project, The Unitarian Rooms, Hoop Lane, London NW11 8BS. Tel: 081 455 8894

The Lesbian and Gay Christian Movement, Oxford House, Derbyshire Street, London E2 6HG. Tel: 071 739 1249; counselling helpline, 071 587 1235.

London Lesbian and Gay Switchboard, tel: 071 837 7324.

The Metropolitan Community Church, BM/MCC, London WC1N 3XX.

The National AIDS Helpline, tel: 0800 567 123.

The National Association of Bereavement Services, 68 Charlton Street, London NW1 1JR. Tel: 071 246 1080.

Quest (for lesbian and gay Roman Catholics), BM Box 2585, London WC1N 3XX. Linkline 071 792 0234 or 041 333 9340.

United States

Affirmation (An organization for gay and lesbian Methodists), Box 1021, Evanston, Ill. 60204. Tel: 708 475 0499.

American Baptists Concerned, 872 Erie Street, Oakland, California 94610 2268. Tel: 415 465 8652.

Dignity (An organization for gay and lesbian Roman Catholics), 1500 Massachusetts Avenue, NW, Suite 11, Washington DC 20005. Tel: 202 861 0017.

Evangelicals Together, Suite 109, Box 16, 7985 Santa Monica Blvd, West Hollywood, California 90046. Tel: 213 656 8570.

Friends for Lesbian and Gay Concerns (An organization for gay and lesbian Friends/Quakers), Box 222, Sumneytown, Pa. 18084. Tel: 215 234 8424.

Integrity (An organization for gay and lesbian Episcopalians), Box 19561, Washington, DC, 20036 0561. Tel: 718 720 3054.

Presbyterians for Lesbian and Gay Concerns, Box 38, New Brunswick, NJ 08903 0038. Tel: 201 846 1510.

Unitarian Universalists for Lesbian and Gay Concerns, 25 Beacon Street, Boston, Mass. 02108. Tel: 617 742 2100.

United Church Coalition for Lesbian and Gay Concerns, 18 N. College Street, Athens, Ohio 45701. Tel: 614 593 7301.

Universal Fellowship of Metropolitan Community Churches, 5300 Santa Monica Blvd, Suite 304, Los Angeles, California 90029. Tel: 213 464 5100.

Europe

Austria

Homosexuelle und Kirche, Österreich, Postfach 513, Ö–1011, WIEN.

Belgium

La Communauté Groupe de Chrétiens Gais, BP 104, B-1000 Bruxelles 1.

Eire

Reach, PO Box 1790, Dublin 6.

France

David et Jonathan, 92 bis Rue de Picpus, F-75017, Paris CCL, 39 Rue de Nantes, F-75019, Paris.

Germany

Homosexuelle und Kirche, Deutschland, Postfach 19 01 65, D-5000, Köln 1

Homosexuelle und Kirche, Deutschland, Oberfeldstrasse 110, D-6000, Frankfurt 50.

Lesben und Kirche, Withrasstrasee 45, D-6000, Frankfurt.

Lesben und Kirche, Teylestrasse 12, D-4630, Bochum.

Holland

LKP-buro, Waterloopln 205, NL-1011 PG Amsterdam.

LKP, Pinksterbloempln 4, NL-2555 EL S Gravenhage.

CHCJ, Postbus 55279, NL-3008 EG Rotterdam.

Stichting de Kringen, Platostraat 142, NL-3076 BP Rotterdam.

Gay European Baptist Federation, Schoolstraat 12, NL-3581 PT Utrecht.

Italy

Gruppo Davide e Gionata, Via Giolitti 21-a, I-10123 Torino.
Gruppo del Guado, Via Pasteur 24, I-20127 Milano.
Gruppo L'Incontro, presso Comunia Evangelica, Corso Milano 6, I-35100 Padova.

Norway

Apen Kirkegruppe, Pastboks 6838, St Olvas Plass N-0130 Oslo 1.

Spain

Cohesion, Apartado 51057, E-28080 Madrid.
Exode, Apartado de Correos 854, E-08080 Barcelona.

Switzerland

Homosexuelle und Kirche, Schweiz, Postfach 7013, CH-8023 Zürich.

Other Countries

Australia

MCC, 109 Maiala Road, Cooks Gap, Mudgee NSW 2850.

Canada

MCC, 409–64 Wellesley Street East, Toronto, Ontario M4Y 1G6.
MCC, 3531 33rd Avenue, Edmonton, Alberta T6H 2G9.

New Zealand

Ascent, PO Box 5328, Dunedin.